HOT
VAMPIRE
NEXT DOOR

SEASON TWO

NIKKI ST. CROWE

BH

BLACKWELL HOUSE

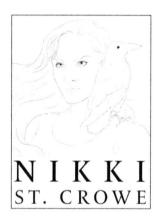

NIKKI
ST. CROWE

Before You Read

Please be aware that Hot Vampire Next Door: Season Two is a boxset of episodes 19-33 of the serial version of the story.

Hot Vampire Next Door is, first and foremost, a serial story published on Vella and is currently ongoing with no scheduled end.

Ebook boxsets will continue to be published for readers who wish to read only as an ebook.

———

Some of the content in this book may be triggering for some readers. If you'd like to learn more about CWs in my work, please visit my website here:

https://www.nikkistcrowe.com/content-warnings

EPISODE NINETEEN
ONLY THE NAUGHTY ONES

YOU TELL YOURSELF A STORY ABOUT WHO YOU ARE and who you're meant to be as you get older.

The story I told myself was that I would pledge to the Locke vampire house just like everyone in my family who had come before me, despite the fact that every time I thought about it, there was a strong hum of dissonance in my gut.

As I got closer to Pledge age, I decided that maybe what I really needed was to leave Midnight Harbor, that I didn't belong there, and no amount of faking it would make it better.

But Bran's words have changed everything I thought I knew about myself and yet...

It almost feels like I've sloughed off a coat that never fit.

Fae.

He tasted fae in my blood.

I'm still naked and dripping his cum down my legs, but my world is spinning and I don't know what to do first.

Clean up or scream.

Bran is beside me in an instant. "Come on." He brings me into the bathroom and wets a rag. "Open up, mouse," he says, nudging my knees apart. He cleans me up with a gentle hand

and I'm so taken aback back by it, so grateful for him, that I'm suddenly teary-eyed.

A fat tear streams down my face and Bran reaches over, swiping it away with his thumb.

"I'm sorry," I say.

"Don't do that."

"What?"

"Don't apologize for your pain."

I nod and then put my face in my hands and suck in several deep breaths.

Bran lets me sit in the silence and the turmoil and it might be the kindest gift anyone has ever given me.

When I feel just slightly more together, I pull my hands away and shove the hair out of my face. He's in the doorway now, my clothes in his hand. I didn't even hear him leave.

"Thank you."

He leaves me to dress.

Once I'm clothed and after several more holy-shit-I-can't-breathe-this-is-insane moments, I leave the bathroom and find Bran at the window staring out into the night. I don't even know what time it is. Everything about my life is twisted and unfamiliar, including my sleep schedule.

"Now what?" I ask. "Where do I go from here?"

My stomach growls, clearly having an opinion on the matter.

Bran looks at me over his shoulder, his gaze on my midsection. "When's the last time you ate?"

I shrug. "I honestly couldn't tell you."

"Then the first thing we'll do is get you some food."

"What, now? I'm not hungry."

He gives me an admonishing glare. "You have to eat, mouse."

"Oh, do I? Oh, thank god you were here. I had no idea that was even a thing mortals did."

He saunters over.

I've always wondered if a vampire has to make considerable effort to walk the speed of us lowly humans, and if so... what does it mean that he's doing it now?

It makes me feel like stalked prey.

Which makes me think he's definitely doing it on purpose.

Using his height, he dominates my personal space so I backpedal, bumping into the wall. His hand comes to my jaw, forcing me to look up at him.

I exhale in a nervous little hiccup.

"You keep talking to me like that, I might have to punish this mouth later."

My tongue darts out, wetting my lips, and he watches the movement with hunger.

"I've only ever given one blow job before," I hear myself saying and then immediately turn red in the face. What the hell? He knew I was a virgin, to a certain degree, but this somehow is more embarrassing. Like I'm freely admitting my deficiencies in the bedroom.

"And?" he says.

"And...it was with Matt Thompson. He said I sucked at it. The pun unintended."

Bran's face darkens. "Matt Thompson is a fucking idiot."

"While I agree with that...I'm just saying...I don't really know what I'm doing in that department."

He dips down and kisses me gently, his mouth lingering on mine. "Don't worry, mouse," he says against my lips. "I'll teach you how."

"Another promise, is it?"

"Mmmm." He reaches up and rubs his thumb over my bottom lip. "I'll look forward to fucking that hole too."

His words send a pulse through my clit. I *am* inexperienced in the bedroom. I know my own pleasure, but I'm realizing there is power in giving pleasure to someone else too.

And maybe that's why Bran loves to control mine. Maybe that's why I love it when he does.

And maybe that's why the thought of giving him something he can't get on his own sends a delicious thrill through my veins.

"Fuck," I say, drawing the word out into several long syllables.

He kisses me again and then he's gone and the air immediately cools with his absence.

"Come on, mouse. It's time to eat." He smirks at me from the door. "You'll need your stamina if you're going to keep up with me."

He doesn't mean in a foot race.

Like a dutiful little mouse, I follow him from the room, down the stairs and out the door.

———

Bran takes me to Crook & Pawn, one of the Duval restaurants. I've literally never stepped foot inside but I've always wanted to. Sam went once with Bianca and described it to me like a New England boarding school on crack.

I never thought I'd get to see it with my own eyes and never on the arm of Bran Duval.

He holds the door open for me and I step inside. There are inset lights in the short entrance hall, giving the space a hushed, soft golden glow. Dark wood covers the walls in the same deep, rich mahogany as the creaky old floor. Oil paintings in gilded frames depicting landscapes and birds and wild horses hang on the wall.

It's the kind of place that instantly brings to mind leather and tobacco and liquor and whispered gossip behind curls of smoke.

There isn't smoking inside, or at least none that I can

smell, but I still get the feeling like there should be or there once was.

We leave the hall, Bran with his hand at the small of my back, me with my head slightly bowed as if I can hide the fact that I come from a Locke family and very much do not belong here.

But as soon as we step foot into the main room, the entire place goes silent save for the classical music playing through the embedded sound system.

Just when I think I understand the silence, that I'm getting used to the kind of attention Bran commands in Midnight, everyone rises from their tables in a cacophony of clattering dishes and chair legs scraping on the wood floor. And then every single person in the room bows their head to Bran.

I look over at him, mouth agape.

There's no emotion on his face. None of the cocky arrogance I'd expect.

Because clearly this happens every single time he steps foot inside the place, and clearly, he's very much used to it.

I know vampire houses and witch covens operate on their own rules, but I never stopped to think just how different one vampire house might be from another.

This level of veneration doesn't exist in the Locke House.

I always knew Bran had a certain level of respect in Midnight Harbor even outside of his house, but I'm not prepared for this. Not at all.

When the bowing and worshipping comes to an end, a hostess hurries over and gives another reverential nod. I can't remember the girl's name, but she's definitely mortal and not too much older than I am. Her attention darts from me to Bran and lingers on him in a way that makes my stomach twist. "Good evening, Mr. Duval. Your usual table?"

"Yes, Merra. Bottle of red too."

"Of course." She leads us through the dining room and all eyes track us. When we reach a back corner booth, Bran motions for me to slide into it. Merra hands me a menu fastened inside a thick leather cover. "I'll be back with the red." She scurries off.

"Mouse," Bran says, his eyes scanning the restaurant. "If you keep gaping at me like that, I might have to find something to put in that pretty mouth."

A shiver races through me and Bran grins.

"You're so funny."

"Yes, I get that a lot. 'You know that Bran Duval, he's such a funny guy.'"

I roll my eyes at him, then, "They're all acting like you're a king."

"I am."

"No, you're not."

"What is a king but a man who declares he's one?"

I frown at him. "That's not how that works."

"I hold the power. They know that."

There's so much about Bran that I've clearly missed over the years.

"And what do you do with all that power?"

He finally looks over at me, his hand finding my thigh beneath the table and squeezing. "I fuck innocent virgin neighbor girls."

I catch more than one person shooting their attention to us, probably eavesdropping on our conversation.

There's no such thing as a secret in a room full of vampires.

If this gets back to Julian...

Not that it should come as a surprise. He did find me half-dressed in Bran's house this afternoon, after all.

"You make it a habit of fucking innocent virgins, do you?" I challenge with a sharp edge of jealousy in my voice.

"Only the naughty ones."

My face flames and I shift on the leather of the booth, thighs rubbing together to ward off the sudden thrill between my legs.

Is it possible to keel over from being horny too often?

There's no such thing as a break when I'm with Bran.

Every touch is electric. Every word edged with innuendo.

Every look molten and ravenous.

We are two storm clouds always threatening to clash.

Merra returns with a wine bottle, but when she pops the cork out and fills a wine goblet, the dark red liquid looks too thick for wine.

Bran immediately drinks it back and runs his tongue over his sharpened fangs, a flare of light coming to his irises.

"What can I get for you?" Merra asks me.

"Oh. Sorry. I didn't even look at the menu." My eyes glaze over the words written in fancy script on the thick paper.

"She'll have a grilled cheese and French fries," Bran answers and takes the menu from me to hand it back. "With a root beer."

"What if I don't want that?"

Bran shoos Merra away with a curt flick of his hand.

"You have a grilled cheese at least three nights a week and always with French fries," he says.

"How would you—"

He taps his nose.

"Right. Of course."

He's not wrong. I do make a lot of grilled cheeses. Kelly doesn't love cooking and neither do I. And judging by the gnawing in my gut, my stomach is here for it.

Merra left the bottle of blood on the table and Bran reaches over to grab it by the neck. The thick liquid glug-glugs as it splashes into the goblet.

"Whose blood is that?" I ask.

He peruses the label. "Says it's Vintage Mitchell Smith, bottled in '79."

"Wait, really?"

I snatch the bottle from him only to find the label mostly blank. It just says, *Red—bottled in Serona with mortal consent.*

He's laughing at me.

"See. You are funny."

He brings the goblet to his lips and takes a tentative sip while his other arm winds behind me along the booth.

A few days ago, I thought he hated me. I thought he couldn't stand the sound of my voice. But now I don't know what to think.

We are inexplicably tangled in one another now, but there's a little voice in the back of my head that keeps reminding me this could all be some grand vampire game just to keep things entertaining in his long, long life.

It makes me want to know. It makes me want to put a magnifying glass to it and dissect it until I can label all its parts and put it in a neat little box.

"What are we doing, Bran?"

His eyes cut to me. "We're having dinner."

"No. I mean...you and me." I lower my voice. "What we just did—"

He cuts me off with his mouth on mine, his arm sliding off the booth, his hand threading through my hair pulling me into him. The kiss isn't long, but it is intimately deliberate.

It feels like a declaration to the entire room.

When he pulls away, my grilled cheese and fries are on the table and Merra is standing by awkwardly, her gaze downcast. "Was there anything else?"

"No," Bran answers. I notice he doesn't say thank you. I suppose the king isn't accustomed to thanking his peasants.

"Thanks, Merra," I say and she nods and darts off.

"Eat, mouse," he tells me, his hand still tangled in my hair but his eyes on the restaurant now. I get the distinct feeling he's waiting for something, biding his time.

Turns out I was right.

I'm nearly finished with my food when the front door bangs open and a figure darts into the restaurant and comes to a sudden stop at our table.

It takes my human eyes a second to focus on the vampire.

Hands on her hips, Sky Carter stands in front of us, boobs revolting against the tight V-neck of her shirt. My stomach sinks.

Sky Carter is fourth in line at the Duval House and worse —she's Bran's ex.

There is a very pointed look on her face. One that could pierce flesh if wielded properly.

"Sky," Bran says in a bored tone of voice.

"You have a taste for trash now, do you?" While she barely looks at me, we all know she's referring to me.

"What do you want?" he asks her.

Is he just going to ignore the fact that she called me trash?

"Damien has summoned you," she answers.

"Try again." His voice rings with authority.

With a sigh, she says, "Damien *asks* that you come to the house."

"Fine."

Sky relaxes. I don't. Bran's body is a hard line beside me, muscles tense.

He is the viper coiling to strike.

I feel the cold air in Bran's absence first. I hear the snap of a neck second.

Sky's eyes roll back in her head as her body thuds heavily to the floor.

I yelp in surprise and the sound rings out in the abrupt silence of the restaurant.

"Come on, mouse." Bran holds out his hand for me and I quickly take it, letting him guide me out of the booth.

As I step over the undead dead body of Sky Carter on the floor, my gut twists.

I will be paying for this later.

Episode Twenty
Death Wish

I can't get comfortable in the bucket seat of the Bimmer.

How could I when Bran is driving us to Duval House in my car where it'll surely get back to Julian Locke?

My Pledging is right around the corner. Instead of the distant annoyance I was feeling about it before, it's now hovering on the horizon like a storm cloud. What will Julian do?

Better yet, what the hell will I do?

Everything has become far more complicated.

"What do you think your brother wants?" I ask.

"With Damien, it's always hard to say." Bran is relaxed in the driver's seat, one hand on the leather steering wheel, the other wrapped around the stick shift.

"And Sky—" I start.

"Don't worry about Sky."

"Easy for you to say. She's not known for showing restraint. You just snapped her neck in the middle of the restaurant because, well...why? Because she called me trash? I'll admit I was really hoping you'd set her straight but—"

"No one is allowed to speak to you that way." His gaze cuts to me quickly before returning to the road. The leather steering wheel groans beneath his grip. "If someone does, you're to tell me."

A thrill blooms in my chest. Kelly has always looked out for me, but not in this live-or-die kind of way. The protection of an older sister is much different than the protection of a vampire like Bran.

"Sky will take it out on me," I say.

"I won't let that happen." He guides the Bimmer off the road and onto the black pavement of the Duval House driveway.

"As if you could stop it. Sky is like a trap-door spider just waiting for the perfect time to pounce."

He laughs.

"I'm serious!"

"I know you are." Another car passes us, the headlights sweeping over his face. "Sky won't hurt you. It wouldn't be worth the risk of my wrath. She knows that."

"Does she?" I ask, frowning at him. "Why would she know that?"

Bran and I have only been fucking around a few days. I don't know why Sky would know anything about me other than the fact that I'm Bran's neighbor and I might annoy him sometimes.

He doesn't look at me as he follows another curve in the driveway.

Duval House finally reveals itself nestled among the hardwoods at the back of a sprawling, well-manicured property.

It's seriously straight out of an English period drama.

Several spotlights are trained on the front of the estate, giving it an ominous feel. Matching flags with the Duval House crest fly from the twin towers on the north and south ends.

Almost every window is lit golden in the night.

Bran ignores the fork of the driveway where the pavement winds back to a parking lot and a six-stall carriage house. Instead, he turns us toward the house and drives beneath an attached porch.

"I wish I was fancy enough to have a drive-thru porch."

"It's called a *porte cochère*."

I like hearing his tongue roll over the French syllables.

I almost tell him to say it again but don't want to look like a simpering dork.

When Bran climbs out, someone is at the driver's side in an instant.

"Come, mouse," Bran calls.

The stranger climbs in behind the wheel and looks at me, waiting.

"What is happening?"

Bran ducks down into the open doorway. "This is Lance. Lance is going to park your car. You are going to get out of the car and follow me. Now, mouse."

Lance gives me an awkward look.

"Be gentle with her, Lance," I say.

He nods. "You have my word, Ms. MacMahon."

Lance knows who I am?

"*Mouse.*"

I scurry out of the car.

There's another guy at the massive double doors, holding one of them open for us.

"This is some white glove service," I mutter.

It makes me wonder again why Bran would ever leave Duval House. It never made any sense. It still doesn't.

The side entrance comes in on a sitting room that must be the size of my entire house. There are wingback chairs and red velvet settees and several leather side chairs positioned in front of a fireplace where a low fire crackles on the bricks.

The people in the room lurch to their feet and bow their heads as we breeze past, but Bran doesn't give them a second look.

We cross a foyer where the black and white marble floor gleams beneath two chandeliers. We pass a grand staircase that has a landing halfway up where the staircase branches off into opposite directions.

When you're a human living in suburbia, it's easy to forget the opulence and the elegance of the supernatural houses. I try not to gape around like a fish out of water as Bran guides me with his hand at the small of my back.

"Why did you leave here?" I blurt out. "This place is amazing."

"It's crowded," he answers distractedly.

"Do you still have a room here?"

"I have many, yes."

"Where?"

"Damien and I shared the north wing."

"The entire wing? How could that possibly get crowded? You probably had more room there than at your house and—"

Bran takes a fistful of my shirt and yanks me to a stop. I bounce off his chest from the sudden shift in momentum, so he hooks an arm around my waist, drawing me back in to keep me on my feet.

"Hey! What—"

Damien is suddenly in front of us.

Damien Duval is the type of man that if I didn't know about the things that go bump in the night and I passed him on a sidewalk, I might think he was a college student studying history or poli sci. He has that kind of air about him, just this side of arrogant and the kind of intelligence that makes most conversations with him hard to keep up with.

I immediately flash back to a few nights ago when I over-head Damien and Bran in Bran's kitchen. Damien was worried about the Lockes throwing their weight around, and thought I might somehow be significant. 'Special' was the word he used.

"Bran," Damien says and then his gaze trails me up and down.

I can't help but shiver beneath the weight of it. Bran yanks me behind him and says, "*No.*" Damien isn't the least bit put off by the threatening rumble in his brother's voice.

"We need to talk." Damien is heading in the opposite direction before I can blink. "Alone," he adds.

Bran sighs.

"What am I supposed to do while you're gone?" I ask and eye the people lingering in the foyer. We're a half-football-field away but I'm sure they can hear us. I don't know if I relish the idea of being alone in the Duval house.

"Jimmy," Bran calls.

A young woman is beside me in a second. "Jessie, hi," she says.

Jimmy, short for Jimena, is currently third in-line at Duval House. In chunky heeled combat boots, she stands several inches taller than me. She smells like rose oil and paint thinner and there is a rainbow of dried paint on her long, brown fingers.

"Look after my little mouse for me," Bran tells her.

"Of course." She smiles down at me with a warm gaze even though I'm absolutely certain she has better things to do.

Bran swivels around and is gone.

"Sorry," I say.

"For what?" Jimmy hooks her arm through mine and steers me away.

"I'm sure babysitting wasn't on your agenda for the night."

"And I'm sure being thrown into the lion's den wasn't on your agenda either." She says the latter with an aye, *aye-ther*.

I've always thought people who pronounce it that way are too fancy for me.

"Everything about the last few days has been unexpected," I mutter.

"So I've heard."

"You have?" I gaze up at her. "What have you heard?"

She guides me through open pocket doors where stained glass is inlaid in the transom windows above. Classical music plays through a sound system while a coffee steamer hisses from the far side of the room.

It's a massive library with a full coffee bar and a winding iron staircase that goes up to the open second-story loft.

"Whoa."

It's so big, and the stacks so plentiful, you could easily get lost in them.

There are work tables set up equidistant from one another on my left. Matching library lamps with pull chains sit on each of the tables and cast golden light around the room. A plush red rug with the Duval crest runs down the center aisle. Six iron chandeliers hang from the vaulted ceiling. There are sitting areas with overstuffed leather chairs dotted around the room.

It's somehow cozy and huge all at the same time.

"Can I get you a coffee?" Jimmy asks. "We have anything you could possibly want."

I follow her to the bar where two humans mix drinks for a couple waiting at the far end.

It's late at night and if I drink coffee, I'll be up till the sun rises, but I guess that might just be my life now.

Though there is a distant nagging voice in the back of my head that reminds me I have a job and a shift to work tomorrow.

"How about tea?"

"Sure." Jimmy leans against the bar. "We have a passion fruit tea." She gives a chef's kiss. "It's excellent."

"I'll take that."

"Scott," she calls and the guy pouring foamed milk into a cup looks up. "Two passion fruit teas, iced, please."

"Coming right up," Scott says.

"So," I say, unsure of exactly *what* to say. I don't belong here and while no one stands and bows like they do when Bran's around, I still get the feeling everyone is whispering about me.

I trail off in a nervous laugh and Jimmy saves me.

"Is Bran being nice to you?" she asks.

I snort. "Does he know how to be nice?"

Jimmy laughs flashing gleaming white teeth. "One of the reasons I aligned myself with Bran and the Duval House when I came to America was because Bran can be both brutal and restrained. He's good at knowing when to push a button, when not to."

Oh, don't I fucking know it.

"Why did you leave your house overseas?" I ask, wanting desperately to move the conversation away from me and my *buttons*.

"Our matriarch died." Jimmy waves her hand dismissively. "It was a long, brutal feud over lovers and cattle, as most vampire wars are." She laughs again. "Anyway, the house started to fall apart afterward. New leadership took over but it wasn't the same. I had known Bran for decades at that point so I asked if he'd have me and he and Damien said yes." She holds her arms out like *voila*. "Here I am."

"Do you like Duval House?"

She scans the library, her long lashes nearly hitting the arched line of her brow. "I do. It's much more structured than the house I came from. More order. On the other hand, I'm a free bird. I don't like being tied down and Bran and Damien have always been good about letting me do my thing when I need to."

I nod at her paint-splattered hand. "Like art?"

She wiggles her fingers. "Art among other things." Her attention wanders to a pretty girl sitting on the arm of a velvet sofa. The girl smiles back. From my vantage point, I can't tell if she's human or vampire. I think human, if I'd have to guess, judging by the looseness to her posture. Vampires always have this edge of alertness to their bodies, as if they could attack at any moment. Or be attacked.

"Jimmy!" someone calls from the pocket doors.

"Stay here at the bar," Jimmy tells me. "This should just take a minute."

Jimmy darts away.

Scott is just scooping ice from a cooler into my cup when the air is disrupted beside me and I turn, thinking it's Jimmy or Bran.

A chill runs down my spine.

It's Sky.

Mother son of a bitch.

It's impossible to tell she was just lying dead on a restaurant floor not that long ago. She's obviously healed. There isn't a bruise anywhere on her skin. There is, however, a very clear thread of disdain on her face.

She reaches over the coffee bar and snatches a bottle of vodka. If I'd known you could get a spiked drink, I might have changed my order.

She twists off the cap and pours two sloshes into a white ceramic mug. She sips from it, keeping her gaze trained on me the entire time.

"Hi Sky," I say. "Nice to see you on your feet."

Internally I cringe. What the hell? Do I have a death wish?

I think having Bran's protection has embolden me, but where is Bran now? Not here. Not here to protect me.

Sky reaches across me and I shrink away like I'm afraid to get burned. She dips her hand inside a large glass canister and pulls out a bag of organic fruit snacks. Except on closer inspection, I see the label mentions they're "made from legally acquired blood."

Blood fruit snacks. I did not know that was a thing.

Sitting on one of the bar stools, Sky crosses one long leg over the other knee and leans back. She tears off a corner from the bag and plucks a bear-shaped gummy from inside, then puts it between her teeth and tears off its head.

The hair rises at the back of my neck.

"Did Bran ever tell you why he left Duval House?" she asks.

If words were ever used as a weapon, Sky has just racked a bullet in the chamber.

Scott sets my tea in front of me. "Enjoy," he says.

I pick it up, swirl the straw inside. The ice clinks together. "I don't think he did, no."

"Mmmm." Sky decimates another bear with the cut of her teeth. "I know why. Do you want to know why?"

Shit.

Yes, I do.

Very much so. It's a question that's plagued me ever since he moved in next door. But I thought the answer might be a bit of drama between him and his brother. Or maybe something political.

Now I have the very distinct impression the answer might gut me.

Sky leans over. Her breath smells like vodka and strawberries as she says, "He left Duval House because of you."

EPISODE TWENTY-ONE
SYNERGY OF GIVE AND TAKE

I AM DISTANTLY AWARE THAT STORMING OFF IN search of Bran in Duval House is more than a little reckless.

I am distantly aware that Sky's admission is as good as her striking a match and lighting the wick of a bomb.

And I'm the bomb.

But right now, I don't care about any of that. There's a knotting in my gut that feels a lot like betrayal.

"Bran!" I yell as I stalk down the hallway. All of the vampires and pledged humans give me a wide berth. "Bran Duval!"

"Jessie." Jimmy is suddenly beside me. "What's wrong?"

"I need to see Bran."

"Okay. But if you'll just—" She cuts herself off, her gaze going distant as if she's listening to something out of range of my hearing. "Bran said to follow me."

"Oh, he did, did he?" She guides me down the hall, then down another and finally shows me into an office where Bran is sitting on the edge of a giant desk. His brother is at the window, a glass of liquor in his hand.

"What's wrong, mouse?" Bran asks, only a slight edge of concern in his voice. "Did someone touch what's mine?"

He means me.

I come to a stop in front of him. Slouched as he is against the desk, we're nearly the same height and the intensity of his stare at eye level causes me to pull to a stop.

"Mouse," he coaxes.

I take in a breath. "Did you leave Duval House because of me?"

His gaze cuts over my shoulder to Jimmy and his face sharpens to a look of reproval.

"It wasn't me," Jimmy answers.

"It was Sky," I say. "And the fact that you're doing that thing with your face tells me all I need to know."

He pushes off the desk and rises to his full height. It makes me feel small and immediately I second guess myself. But no. *No.*

"Mouse," he says with warning.

"Why?" I shove a finger in his chest. "Why haven't you told me? And why would you do that? That doesn't make any sense."

"That's what I told him," Damien says to the window.

"Why, Bran?"

"That's a very long story." His voice is low and throaty.

"I have time."

"Mouse."

We face off silently and stoically for several long seconds. Bran is stubborn. But I can be too.

"You promised me you'd always tell me the truth. Last chance."

He still says nothing.

Decision made, I swivel on my heel and turn to Jimmy. "Could you please show me the way to my car?"

Her eyes dart to Bran and then, "Sure. Of course."

I can feel Bran's attention on me as I leave the room. He doesn't try to stop me. Good thing too, because I'm *this close* to punching a vampire in the face.

———

Jimmy walks me across the Duval property and shows me to my car. The keys are tucked in the visor—a very obvious place for keys to be. No one would dare steal a car from Duval property, though, so I suppose I'm not miffed about it.

"Thank you," I tell Jimmy as I slide in behind the wheel.

She comes into the open driver's side door and says, "Try not to be too hard on him. He often does what he does out of love."

I snort. "I think what you mean is he does it because he thinks he's better than everyone else and he thinks he can get away with doing whatever he wants."

She doesn't argue that. "Be careful, okay? Bran would lose his shit if something happened to you."

I roll my eyes. "I don't think that's true."

"Just...promise me, okay?"

"Fine. Sure. I will obey all traffic laws."

She steps back and I slam the door shut and crank the engine over, feeling just slightly guilty for taking out my annoyance on Jimmy.

I roll down the window and say, "Thank you."

She nods and, in an instant, she's gone.

———

I half expect to find Bran on my front porch when I get home, but he isn't there.

I park in the driveway and go inside. The house is dark and

quiet. Kelly still isn't home? I go upstairs and find her bed made and unrumpled so I shoot her a quick text.

Where are you?

Locke House comes her quick reply.

Not that long ago, talking to my sister about my Pledging and my childhood seemed like the most important thing, but now? Shit is piling up and I don't even know where to start anymore.

Why the hell would Bran leave Duval House for me? Clearly Damien knew about it. Which explains why I heard the rumor they got into a fight over him leaving.

I decide the best thing to do is take a shower, scrub the night and Bran from my skin, and then try to sleep somewhat normal hours. But as I'm padding down to the kitchen for a bottle of water in nothing but my robe, I hear a knock on the back door.

I know who it is before I pull it open.

I find Bran with an arm propped on the door frame, leaning into the open doorway as much as the magic of invitations will allow.

I don't know what that strange magic is or what governs it, but it works better than any charm.

Bran will never be able to cross that threshold without being invited by myself or Kelly.

"What do you want?" I ask.

"I came to explain."

"I'm listening." I cross my arms over my chest and Bran watches as the silk material of my robe rides up on my bare thighs.

"If I tell you," he says, his gaze finally returning to my face, "it might change things between us."

"You not telling me has clearly changed things between us."

I can feel the power shifting. He's treating this whole thing like a scale of justice. One wrong move and the scales will tip. Right now what we have going on is a delicate balance of control, a synergy of give and take. If I'm being honest, I'm afraid of the scales shifting too, but I need to know.

"Invite me in," he says, "and I'll tell you."

I laugh, but it's more derision than humor. "I'm not doing that."

"Mouse."

"Tell me."

"I'm not telling you when I can't get to you."

"Why?" I cock out a hip. The robe slips again. "Because you know that if you can just touch me, tease me, *control* me, maybe the truth won't be so bad for me to hear?"

He doesn't answer, but the sharpened edge to his expression tells me I've nailed it.

I exhale, uncross my arms. He watches the robe again.

And an idea comes to me.

It's as much about me taking back some control as it is about getting revenge.

I go upstairs.

"Mouse!" he calls.

I come back a minute later with my favorite bunny vibrator. It's a deep violet shade made of silicone with an innie and an outie point of contact so I can fuck myself and hit my clit at the same time.

It's gotten me off more times than I can count.

Bran's gaze sinks to it in my hand and then he narrows his eyes.

"Mouse." His voice reverberates with warning.

"Last chance."

"I'm not playing games," he says.

Well, I am.

And I'm about to take this one home.

I settle myself into the doorway just this side of the

threshold and prop my foot on the other side. The robe parts, exposing me, and Bran's nostrils flare.

I am a responsible owner of toys and always wash mine after use, so when I pop it in my mouth, I know it's nice and clean.

Bran growls in the back of his throat as I close my eyes and fuck my mouth with it, getting it nice and wet.

When I pull it out, I let my lips pop around it.

Bran's eyes are glowing now.

I readjust, hit the ON button and the toy vibrates in my hand.

Bran's breathing intensifies as I drag the toy over my pussy. I might have been anticipating the sensation, but the way Bran leans in, teeth gritted, makes the pleasure sink a little deeper.

I arch against the doorframe and slip the vibrator inside my slick channel.

"Oh fuck," I moan for dramatic effect but when I increase the pace and Bran puts his hands on his side of the door frame and the wood groans around his grip, the pleasure pounds through me like a summer storm.

I keep fucking myself, the soft nubby end hitting my clit with every thrust.

The tie on the robe slips open and my nipple hits the cool air, beading to a peak.

Bran bites at his bottom lip, drawing blood. His dark brow is sunk into a deep V as he mops up the blood with a swipe of his tongue.

I moan again.

"Mouse," he says, his voice low and throaty.

"I bet you wish it was you inside of me."

Whoa. Where did that come from?

But I immediately see the teasing has hit him exactly where I intended.

There's a very clear bulge at the front of his pants.

I fuck myself a little harder and hit the button for more intense vibration. The sensation pulses through me and there's a very distinct wet sound coming from my pussy now.

I groan and pant and groan again as the orgasm rises, rises, the nub hitting my throbbing clit just right.

"Oh...fuck..." I pant out and then capture my nipple between two fingers, rolling it for a stroke of pain.

As the orgasm takes hold and I cry out, the doorframe groans beneath Bran's grip and the wood cracks.

The pleasure roars through me like a forest fire, consuming my veins, pulsing and thrilling every hollow corner of my body. My thighs quiver and I arch, knees trembling as I hold the toy deep inside, the nub tight against my clit as several aftershocks pound through me.

When I come down and refocus, I find Bran staring at me with two eyes like embers.

I've never seen so much pain and anguish on his face before.

The doorframe groans again, his knuckles white.

I pull the vibrator out, and then drag my tongue over my juices glistening on the violet shaft.

"Mmmm," I say. "So sweet."

"You'll pay for this one, little mouse." The rumble is gone from his voice. Now he is cold and distant.

It sends a shiver down my spine and a new pulse through my pussy.

I know I will. But for right now, I'm high on the orgasm and the victory. I needed to take back some of my own power just to prove to him and myself that I could.

"Stop fucking keeping shit from me," I say, and grab hold of the back door, "and maybe next time you can join me."

Then I slam the door in his face.

Episode Twenty-Two

Obey Me

I just slammed the door in Bran's face.

He's going to get my ass for that one but for now I'm safe and sound in my own home and I'm gonna soar on this win for as long as I can. I fucking earned it.

Up in my bedroom, I hesitate just outside the square of moonlight pouring through my bedroom window. I haven't turned on the overhead light yet, so I can easily see across the valley between my house and Bran's.

His window is dark.

I quickly snap my curtains shut and then get ready for bed, thinking I'll sleep like a baby.

Wrong. I toss and turn all night with this constant nagging desire to go to my bedroom window and peek through the curtains to see if Bran is there, to see if his bedroom light is on.

Somehow, I manage to stay beneath my quilt until my phone tells me it's just after seven in the morning. I think I slept some, but not enough judging by the heaviness in my eyes and the ringing in my ears.

I pull on a pair of leggings and pass my bedroom window

and find myself lingering in the slant of pale blue light stealing through the crack in the curtains.

I can't help myself. I reach out and pull one back a few inches.

My heart sinks. Bran's blinds are shut tight. Not that I should be surprised. It is morning, after all, and vampires hate mornings. He'll be sleeping for the rest of the day.

Which is just as well because I have a life to return to and a shift at the coffee shop to work. But I'd be lying if I said I wasn't excited about what might happen when day falls and night breaks.

Bran will come looking for me. Of that I'm absolutely sure.

Just thinking about his promise before I slammed the door in his face has my skin prickling and my nerves lighting up.

You'll pay for this one, little mouse.

Oh, the things Bran Duval promises to do to me in the dark. It's enough to keep that teasing flame at my clit flickering long after it should have died out.

I hate the way he can sway me like that, but damn if I don't love the rush it gives me.

I haven't felt this much *in my skin* in...well, ever.

In the kitchen, I get the coffee maker going and then return to my bathroom to scrub my face and throw on some makeup. I only bother with mascara, a brush of blush, and a swipe of tinted chapstick. With freckles, I've always thought it was pointless to wear concealer or foundation. I like my freckles. Let them shine.

Returning to the kitchen, I find the coffee maker has done its job and steam is rising from the pot and curling in the sunlight shining through the kitchen window. I find my favorite travel mug in the dishwasher and fill it up, add some creamer, and screw on the top. I still have forty-five minutes before I'm supposed to be at work but if I stay here any longer, I'm worried about what I might do.

I could probably walk in Bran's front door and up to his bedroom and slip into his bed and—

Nope. Nope.

To work it is.

Climbing in behind the wheel of the Bimmer while the dew burns off of the grass feels familiar, and I take in a deep breath of the fresh morning air, then exhale.

Everything is going to be all right.

————

Rita is behind the counter when I walk into Magic Coffee Shop. She looks up when the bell dings, announcing my arrival. Her dark brow sinks over her brown eyes. "What are you doing here?"

"I'm scheduled to work today." I hang my bag on the hook in the back and then tie on one of the waist aprons with the Magic Coffee Shop logo embroidered in rainbow thread on the hip.

Rita's frown deepens.

"What?" I say.

"It's just..." She licks her lips and tucks her pen into her top knot of braids. "Why don't you take the day off? I know you have a lot going on and—"

"Rita, I want to be here." I sigh and scrub at my face. "No, I think what I mean is, I *need* to be here. Is that okay? I want to just work and clear my head and be normal for a second."

She purses her lips together and regards me with the warm, concerned look of a mother. Finally, she nods. "I was planning on being here for the morning anyway, so I'll catch up on some paperwork and maybe pop down to the supply store after the lunch rush."

"Sounds perfect."

As she passes me for her office in the back, she wraps her hand around my arm and squeezes. I catch the scent of her oil blend—patchouli and lemongrass and lavender. "If you need me, you just call for me, okay?"

"Sure. I'll be fine. I promise."

With a nod, she lets me go and disappears in back.

It isn't long before the shop is full and I'm so busy, I don't have a spare minute to dwell on all the shit going wrong in my life. It's absolute bliss.

Gwen, a witch barista who works at the shop, shows up for her afternoon shift a little after two, so when my best friend Sam walks in the door at half-past-three, I can take a little break to chat with her.

After a quick hug, she sits on a stool at the counter and grabs a honey stick from the display cup. "Where the hell have you been?" She reaches over the counter for the scissors and clips off the end of the stick. Honey oozes out the end and she licks it off.

"You won't believe me if I told you," I answer.

"Yes, I would. Because you don't lie."

I pull to a stop and frown at her.

"What?" she says.

Fae can't lie. I don't lie on principle, but I *have* lied in the past. Like that time Principal Manwell caught me skipping class and I told him my sister had an emergency which was totally not true.

But...how can that be? Fae can't lie. That's like written in the fae canon or whatever.

Maybe Bran was wrong. Thinking this, thinking I have an out, fills me with so much damn relief I nearly weep.

"Jess," Sam prods. "Why do you have that dumb look on your face?"

I arch a brow at her and she laughs.

"I just realized something is all. Anyway..." I fill one of the portafilters with freshly ground espresso and tamp it down. "I've been with Bran Duval."

Sam clamps her teeth on the honey stick as her eyes get big. "Okay. Okay. Definitely didn't expect that twist, but I'm here for it," she says. "Go on."

I twist the filter into the espresso machine and push the button to brew. The machine churns to life.

"It all started after Kelly showed up with this nasty bite on her neck," I say.

"I've clearly missed so much."

As I make Sam her favorite frappe, I fill her in on *most* of the details, but have to leave out a few key points considering anyone in the coffee shop could be listening in with their supernatural hearing.

I don't tell Sam about the mind-bending sex with the infamous Bran Duval. I can dish all those details later.

"Here's where things get a little wild," I tell her as I slide the frappe over the counter. "Are you ready for it?"

She upends the rest of the honey stick into the cup. "I've had the most boring twenty-four hours compared to yours, so yes. Mom sent me to Mulligan House for a celebration ritual that amounted to a turkey dinner and a bonfire for burning our fears." She rolls her eyes. "I don't know if I'm cut out for being bound to a witch house. I find all of the rituals and ceremonies"—she lowers her voice and leans in—"*insufferable*. So go on, I could stand for some excitement even if it's not mine."

"Okay, well...Bran bit me and—"

"He what?!"

"And he said he tasted something different in my blood."

"He...*what*?"

I want to tell her exactly what he thinks he tasted in my blood but again...*ears*.

"And then I found out when I went to Duval House with

him that he supposedly left the house because of me. And now he won't tell me why. How the hell does that make any sense?"

Sam puts her head in her hands. "I'm trying to compute all of this and it's not working."

"Welcome to my Shit Show, Sam. Pull up a chair and pour a stiff drink, because it's wild in here."

"You aren't kidding." She sits with the information for a second and then sips from her frappe. "Okay. So. First thing...he bit you. What did he taste?"

I scan the people in the shop. Most are absorbed in their own conversations, but a few people are alone with their devices.

"He has a theory, but...hold on." I pull out my cell phone and bring up the text window. I hit Sam's name and type up a message that says: *he thinks he tasted fae blood.*

My heart drums a little harder as my thumb hovers over the SEND button. Being with Bran and being inside his world sorta feels like a dark fairy tale. And in that dark fairy tale, it's not that big of a deal, the girl finding out she has fae blood running through her veins.

But out here in my normal life, telling Sam will somehow make it very, very real.

Sam widens her eyes at me, telling me to hurry up.

I send the message with a deep breath and Sam's phone pings a second later. When she opens and reads the message, she nearly falls off her stool. She grabs at the counter at the last second and the stool knocks back to the floor.

"WHAT?!" she says too loudly.

Several heads turn our way.

"Shhh!"

"WHAT?" she repeats, still clutching at the counter.

"I know it sounds crazy."

"Crazy? Ha. Ha!"

"Are you okay?"

She gives me a look. "After you dropped that asteroid? I mean! How...but...okay...*he*...*you*...do you believe him?"

I left out the part about Sasha and her bite because that's a giant secret that isn't entirely mine to tell.

The Sasha information is a thorn in my side that I can't seem to pluck out. The secret about her biting me and then "disappearing" didn't come from Bran. It came from Runa and Cal. It's much harder to ignore proof when it comes from multiple sources.

"I honestly don't know what to believe at this point," I tell Sam. "I suspect Kelly has been avoiding me and she's the only person who might be able to shed more light on it."

"Your Pledging is two days away," Sam points out.

I collapse against the back counter and let out a sigh that sends my bangs fluttering over my forehead. "I know."

"What if Damien bids on you? Are you going to accept it?"

If I joined Duval House, I'd have to leave my home and the only other place I could go would be Duval House, which would put me further away from Bran. Unless...would he come back?

Is that even what I want at this point?

Once you accept a bid and Pledge yourself to a House, there's no backsies. That's a decision you make for life. I have to be careful about what I do, if I do anything.

I could still leave Midnight.

But thinking about leaving immediately brings to mind Bran in his bed, pleading with me not to go.

And going doesn't hold the same allure it did.

One very hot, very annoying vampire has taken that place.

Everything about Bran is a whirlwind, a chaos storm, and I'm swept up inside of it.

I hate him and I'm pissed at him and yet...I can't get enough of him.

"Jessie!" Sam snaps her fingers in my face. "What are you going to do?"

"I—"

The bell above the door rings out. Instinctively, I turn to the customer to greet them, but the air gets lodged in my throat and no words can find their way out.

The one and only very hot, *very* annoying vampire is standing in a triangle of sunlight in the doorway. Smoke rises from his shoulders and curls in the light. Dark sunglasses shield his eyes, but I know he's looking right at me.

Vampires very rarely come out before five p.m. Too much UV light. Too much risk of spontaneously combusting.

But Bran isn't just any vampire. And he's not here for an afternoon jolt of caffeine.

"Get your keys," he tells me.

"I'm working."

"Get your keys and get in the car, mouse." His voice rumbles with authority.

Sam looks between me and Bran at the door. The rest of the coffee shop does the same. This is a reality TV show taking place right in front of their eyes.

What will the girl do?

I fold my arms over my chest. "And what if I don't?"

What I expect him to do is lay out some minor threat that could also be construed as a sexual punishment. I'm almost looking forward to it. I pretty much asked for this, didn't I? I'm the kid testing out the outlet with the pointy tines of a fork.

But what Bran says instead catches me off guard and makes my heart drop to my feet.

"If you don't, then I'll leave Midnight right now and never come back."

And here I thought I had the upper hand. I was wrong yet

again. Bran isn't a storm I'm caught up in. He is the sun and I am involuntarily drawn to him, stuck in his gravitational pull.

I won't refuse him. I can't. I don't want to, knowing what the consequence will be.

And he knows it.

He's found my weakness and now he's making me admit to it. As much to him as to myself.

"Jess?" Sam says.

"Looks like I have to go." I untie my apron. "Gwen, are you good?"

The witch nods at the other end of the counter. "I'm good."

I grab my bag from the back and give Sam a quick hug. "I'll call you later?"

"You better." She eyes Bran over my shoulder. He's still smoking in the sunlight but he hasn't flinched.

How long before a vampire bursts into flames?

How long before I smolder in his wake?

When I reach him, I'm faced with my reflection in the lenses of his sunglasses. They're so dark, I can't see his eyes, but I can feel the weight of his stare.

"After you," he says.

I step out into the light and fish the keys from my bag. We cross the street together, leaving a trail of smoke behind us. Bran is oddly calm about the whole thing, considering he's walking tinder at this point.

At the Bimmer, Bran stops at the trunk. "Open it, mouse." I fumble with the keys and get the one I need trapped in the ring of my *Dude Where's My Car?* keyring. "Hurry, mouse."

I finally get it untangled and pop the trunk. Bran shoves aside my bag of jumper cables and bungee cords and climbs in.

"What are you doing?"

"Drive until sunset," he orders, a very clear thread of anger reverberating in his voice.

"Are you—"

He grabs the trunk and slams it closed, sealing him inside. Smoke wafts out in a plume, causing me to cough. You'd think it'd smell like burning flesh, but there's only the faintest hint of spice and ash.

"Okay then." I wave the smoke away and climb in behind the wheel.

———

I drive in circles for what feels like hours. I decide to take some of my favorite roads, the narrow lane that winds along Midnight Lake where the houses are practically built on top of each other, each vying for a view of the water.

I head north after that and pass a few of the farms on the outskirts of Midnight, where the farmers not only deal in eggs and beef, but also in blood for the few vampires in town who choose to go the animal route instead of the human one.

As the sun descends below the treetops, I'm way back in the woods on a dirt road.

It's here that my trunk pops open.

I glance at the rear-view mirror for only a second, but when I look back at the road, Bran is there in the weak beam of my headlights, his shirt charred at the shoulders.

"Christ!" I slam on the brakes. The tires skid over the gravel and I have to whip the wheel around just to stay on the road.

I finally come to a stop and throw the car into park.

"What the hell are you doing?" I yell. "I could have crashed my car!"

Bran stalks to the driver's side door and rips it open.

"Hey!"

He grabs me by the arm and yanks me out, spins me

around and slams me over the hood. I huff out a breath, hands braced on the warm metal as the engine continues to run.

"What are you—"

There's a clank of metal, a snap of leather, and a second later, my arms are crossed over my back and tied at the wrists with Bran's leather belt.

He bends over me with all of his weight, his groin at the swell of my ass. "Are you listening now, mouse?"

My heart is slamming against my ear drums. "Yes."

I have a safe word. I could use it if I needed to.

"I have very little respect for human life," he admits. "And even less patience for games."

"I thought we were—"

His hand curls around my throat as his mouth comes to the curve of my ear. "Quiet, little mouse. It's my turn to speak."

I swallow hard. His grip tightens.

"I operate on a very thin line," he says. "With you, I try very, very hard to control myself." His voice rumbles. He's suddenly thick and hard at the seam of my ass. "But that control has its limits. If you want this, little mouse, you only get it one way. *My* way. Do you understand me?"

My pussy throbs. "Yes."

The pressure of his weight disappears and I'm just exhaling with relief when he yanks my pants down, baring me, and cracks me across the ass.

"Ouch! What the—" I wiggle against the car, but Bran presses his free hand at the small of my back, locking me in place. He spanks me again, hard, and a sharp thrill pulses through my pussy as the pain radiates across my cheek.

He takes up a length of my hair and wraps it around his hand, yanking my head back. "Will you obey me?"

I pant out a breath. I'm suddenly throbbing and wet.

Say what you want about Bran Duval, he knows all of the buttons to push.

I'm over here playing checkers and he's launching a fucking rocket ship.

"I will only ask you this once. Yes or no, mouse?" His other hand follows the curve of my ass, his fingers trailing devilishly close to my slick opening. Instinctively I push into him and he pulls my hair harder.

"Yes," I say.

"Yes what?"

Every day, you're faced with choices. Do you want almond milk or oatmilk? The red shoes or the black ones?

Sometimes the choices are life-altering, like this one.

Sometimes it'll change you irrevocably and your life will branch off in an entirely different direction.

This is that choice.

I can feel the tremor of it at the center of me. A seismic shift.

I will never be the same after Bran Duval.

I will never be the same after this choice. It's throwing everything I thought I knew about myself into question.

And yet...and yet...

There is now a spotlight on what I want and what I need and I know it includes Bran as much as he frustrates and annoys me.

I don't know why. I don't know what it says about me to like this so damn much, but if I don't look too closely at it, maybe I'll come out the other side unscathed.

"Yes," I say, "I'll obey you."

"Good girl." He spins me around. "Now get on your knees."

Episode Twenty-Three

Open Up, Mouse

I asked for this.

I said I would obey Bran because I want all the sinful things he's promised to do to me in the dark.

I want to feel the pleasure of his punishments and the pain of his control.

I want to feel the power that comes with all of it. The power of giving in to him and to the desires of my own damn body.

He watches me expectantly, waiting. His patience only goes so far.

I sink to the ground. Gravel bites at my knees. He reaches down and brushes the hair away from my face, then drags his thumb over my bottom lip.

With his other hand, he unzips his pants. My heart kicks up expectantly and my tongue flicks out, wetting my mouth.

His hardness bulges at his boxer briefs. If my hands weren't still tied behind my back, I might reach out to stroke it, feel him strain against the material.

He pulls the waistband down and his cock comes out,

heavy and thick. He takes it in his hand and gives it several pumps.

I inhale deeply. I already admitted to him that I don't know how to give a good blow job. Last night I fucked myself with a vibrator right in front of him. I knew what I was doing last night, and I was soaring high on that confidence.

Now...I'm a little sick with nerves. What if I do it wrong? I've given so much of myself to him already, but I don't want to look like the inept mortal girl I know I am. Especially next to him.

The head of his cock swells in the cuff of his hand. "Open up, mouse," he orders.

I lick my lips again and swallow hard.

"I don't really know—"

He shoves his cock in, catching me off guard. There's no time to think about it now.

He pumps into me and I exhale roughly through my nose.

He's hard as a rock, filling my mouth. I flatten my tongue, trying to find room for him as the head of his cock throbs in the back of my throat.

Taking a length of my hair, winding it around his fist, he pulls my head back and his cock out.

"Breathe," he says and I gasp for air as tears well in my eyes. "Good girl." Then he shoves back in, pumps harder as he groans above me. There's a tortured thrill building between my legs, and butterflies in my belly as he uses me for his own pleasure.

The head of his shaft throbs on the back of my tongue as he pushes in further. I gag, but he continues his assault, growling around gnashed teeth.

"Fuck, your mouth feels so fucking good."

A warm flush comes to my cheeks. He's breathing harder now, and his grip on my hair tightens as he angles me up.

"Look at me, mouse. I want to see you when I come in your mouth."

When I meet his gaze, tears streaming down my face, his eyes glow amber in the semi-darkness and his fangs sharpen.

"Fuck," he grunts out. "You will be my undoing." He drives deeper as if punishing me for it. As if he can't get enough of me.

And just when I think I can't take much more, he growls loudly and spills his hot seed down my throat.

I'm not ready for it and I let out a strangled sound around his thickness.

His cum is coppery and salty and when he pulls out of me, I move to spit it out.

"No." He clamps his hand over my mouth. "Swallow it."

Several beads of cum sit on my tongue as his gaze burns into me.

Another order I can't refuse and the authority in his voice makes me burn hotter with need.

I swallow it back and the taste of him fills my mouth.

"Good girl," he says and then lifts me up, presses me against the car's front fender.

Please fuck me now, I think.

I'm mindless, spinning, buzzing with need. Being used is apparently another one of my kinks. My clit is throbbing, my nipples are tight, and I'm so wet, it's dripping down my inner thighs.

I'm burning and mascara is probably running down my face, but I need more of him.

I want all of him.

"You made me another promise," I say, voice thin, almost a whimper.

He once told me he'd bend me over the hood of my car.

I want that to happen right now.

Bran drags his thumb roughly over my bottom lip. "When

I bend you over the hood, I won't be fucking this hole." Then his hand sinks between my legs where my panties are still askew. He slips his fingers down my wetness, then teases at my opening and I mewl at the pleasure, rocking my hips against him. "And I won't be fucking this hole."

My eyes shoot open. "What?"

"I'm going to fuck that tight ass and you're going to take it like a good girl."

"But—"

"Mouse."

There's a very clear ring of warning in his voice.

"Okay," I say a little breathy, even though I'm not absolutely sure what I'm agreeing to. In all my own pleasure, I've never gone down that road.

"That's the right answer." He zips up his pants and then reaches around me to unknot his belt from my wrists.

"Wait...but..."

"Get in the car." He goes to the driver's side door, the belt hanging from his grip.

"But I...you can't..." I'm still throbbing and soaked.

"You don't get to come," he tells me. "Not until I say you can. Now get in the car." He slides in behind the wheel and shuts the door.

Fuck. Fuck!

I breathe heavily, trying to think through my options. But of course, I don't have many.

"Mouse," he says. "I won't tell you again."

He'll probably leave me here. He already did it once in the cemetery and town is a lot farther away from here. I'd be walking all night.

I fix my pants and numbly walk around the car. Every step is torture as the friction from my panties hits just right at my swollen clit.

Goddamn him.

I carefully climb into the passenger seat, thighs pressed together, trying to stave off the needy heat between my legs.

I want to murder him.

"You're doing this just to torture me," I tell him.

He puts the car in gear and pulls away from the shoulder. "Do you remember what I told you the night you went to the Harbor party?"

I think I know what he's getting at.

When I don't answer, he goes on. "I told you not to wear panties and you didn't. I told you I did it to test your obedience. It wasn't to torture you, mouse." He glances at me briefly, his eyes catching the light from the dashboard. "I did it to teach you the lines not to cross. Disobeying me is one of them. And testing my patience is not something either of us wants."

My stomach dips. Am I flying too close to the sun?

Do I have no idea what I've gotten myself into?

"Should I be afraid of you?" I ask.

"Absolutely." He comes up to a stop sign and looks over at me again, his gaze lingering on me this time. "You can trust me to keep my word, however. So long as you keep yours."

He means as long as I obey him.

I already said I would. I don't plan on backtracking now. But there's clearly so much I have yet to learn. Every second of this relationship is a walk across a tightrope.

I had no idea that before Bran, I was just surviving.

Now I'm living.

The danger, the pleasure, the control, the thrill of it all, it is intoxicating and I'm officially addicted.

"What about my safe word?" I ask. "I can still use it at any time?"

"Yes, but don't think of it as a pause button. Think of it as a ripcord." He turns onto the next street and shifts through several gears as we hit a straightaway and the Bimmer picks up speed. The velocity presses me against the bucket seat.

"Are you saying that when I use the safe word, that's it? We're done?"

"I'm saying I won't know until you use it."

Well, goddammit. That makes me not want to use it. I'm glad I haven't yet.

Because the truth is, the thought of not having Bran anymore makes me feel hollow.

We are tangled in one another now and I think it's that way for him too, as much as it is for me. It's why he's working so damn hard to draw the lines and make sure I know where they are.

Through the control, he's revealing his deepest secret—he doesn't want this to end either.

Bran Duval likes me.

He might *more* than like me.

It might be immature to think about it that way, but it still sends butterflies flitting through my stomach, nonetheless.

The Infamous Bran Duval, a several-hundred-year-old vampire, likes me.

I smile to myself.

Bran says, "Why are you smiling?"

"No reason."

"Mouse."

Am I disobeying him by not telling him all of my inner thoughts? I have to leave some of the mystery.

"I was just thinking I like this song," I say as an 80s pop ballad plays through the radio.

"Liar."

I laugh to myself and then—

"Wait. You're right. I am lying. I forgot to tell you...I realized today that I can lie."

He frowns and downshifts as we reach our next turn. "That is…interesting."

"See! I knew it meant something. Fae can't lie."

He checks for traffic at the stop sign and then turns, the headlights sweeping across the front of Midnight Library and its dark stained-glass windows.

"Try it again," he says. "Tell me an obvious lie."

"I like you," I say with a sardonic grin.

He cuts a look to me. "Mouse."

"Okay. Okay." It wasn't a lie anyway. "It's morning." I spread my arms out. "See?"

His frown deepens. There's a special kind of satisfaction that comes with baffling Bran.

"I know what I tasted in your blood," he says. "I wasn't mistaken."

"You had to be."

"I suppose it's possible the binding amulet has muddled the taste of your blood."

The absolute relief I feel when he says as much is damn near orgasmic.

It's like everything has been put back in place. I don't have to doubt who I am.

"Maybe Sasha said she tasted fae blood too, but was mistaken just like you. Maybe Julian Locke thinks I'm fae, but I'm not."

"But why bind you then?" he points out. "What was your mother trying to hide?"

Okay, he has me there. "Well…I don't know."

"Exactly. I'll admit, the lying is a wild card I didn't consider until now. But it's not a nail in the coffin, so to speak." He's quiet for a second, then, as if making a decision, takes a sharp right turn.

"Where are you going?"

"We need to speak to your sister. Let's not delay it any longer. I want answers and she can give them to us."

"My house is the other way."

"She's not home."

"How do you know?"

"She called in sick today and I heard she's been staying at Locke House."

I swallow around a lump in my throat.

Bran takes the next left turn, ignoring the blinker. "I suspect Julian has been keeping Kelly from you ever since he found you with me."

I've been desperate to speak to my sister and now that I might actually get the chance? I'm afraid of what she might reveal.

I'm afraid of what the truth might be.

My mom did go to an awful lot of trouble to keep secrets about me hidden.

It's possible that I'm going to look back on this and realize that being fae was the least of my worries.

Episode Twenty-Four

Playing with Fire

Locke House is a bit of a misnomer, since the property isn't just one house but two. The Second Residence, as it's called, was added to the property in 1941 when Locke House took in several widows who lost their husbands to WWII.

My maternal great-grandmother was one of those women.

My mom used to brag about that fact to anyone who would listen, even though every citizen of Midnight Harbor already knew the story of the war widows.

Julian's decision to take in charity cases was looked upon with reverence and admiration.

I was never so sure. Sometimes I secretly thought Julian saw the war widows, my great-grandmother included, as easy prey.

Unlike my dad's family that had been bound to the Locke House for over two centuries, my mom's family were outsiders. Meaning they had no idea the supernatural world existed until they were brought into it.

The Second Residence had tried to match the original house's Italianate architecture but never came close enough.

It's just a white box with some decorative black trim and a wide front porch with simple, straight columns.

The main house, however, was always supposed to be the center of attention.

It was constructed in the mid-1800s by some renowned architect that I can never remember the name of. The house is overly designed with decorative cornices and multiple towers and a front door so big you could drive a truck through it.

And it honest-to-god has a room called the belvedere because it overlooks the pond at the back of the Locke property.

Kelly and I used to joke that our dining room was the belvedere because it had a clear view of the other neighbor's trash cans.

"Dinner is ready!" she'd call up to me. "Meet me in the belvedere."

No matter how many times we used the joke, it was always funny.

The first edge of worry comes over me, thinking about Kelly. I've been so wrapped up in my own shit that I didn't take enough time to properly check in on my sister since the bite.

With the worry is guilt.

Bran parks the Bimmer in the lot behind the Second Residence. Unlike at Duval House, there's no Lance waiting beneath a *porte cochère* to valet my car for me.

Locke House might have a belvedere, but I'm beginning to realize most of what Julian does, he does for show. Duval House is bougie as fuck, but it's casual wealth. The Duvals don't show off. They just *are* rich and surrounded by luxury because it's who and what they are.

They don't even have to try.

When we walk out from the parking lot, there are several vampires and a few humans milling around the side garden that stretches between Second Residence and Locke House. Cody and François are the only two who come forward. They've been together since 1969 when François changed Cody at Woodstock.

François has his arm draped over Cody's shoulders. He's taller than Cody by several inches, though he's given an extra few for the height of his frohawk.

Cody is dressed in brown jeans and a short sleeve button-up shirt with pearl snaps. I don't think he ever left Woodstock. His feet are bare.

"Jessie," François says, giving me a friendly nod. "'Tis a brave move, bringing a Duval here."

Even though it's been several centuries since François left France, some of his accent still comes through.

"There's no rule against it, is there?" I ask.

"I suppose not."

"Is my sister here?"

"She is," François answers.

"In the main house," Cody adds.

I can't shake the feeling that they're hiding something from me.

"How has she been since that horrible bite the other night?"

Cody and François share a look. "We know nothing of a bite," François answers.

"Mmm. Well, Julian said he'd handle it so maybe he did. But Kelly came home the other night with her throat torn. Bran had to heal her."

Cody threads his fingers with François's hand that hangs over his shoulder. "We didn't know anything about that, Jess. Honestly."

I give them a nod. "Okay, well...we're going to head in then."

"I'd leave the Duval outside," François suggests.

Bran mimics François and hangs his arm casually over my shoulders. "*The Duval* will go where Jessie goes."

It's weird hearing him say my name.

I don't like it.

The guys regard me with an equal measure of worry and surprise.

"Your funeral," François says to Bran.

Bran says nothing.

We leave the guys and follow the paved walk from the Second Residence up the gentle hill to Locke House. Bran removes his arm from around me and I immediately miss the weight of his nearness.

I don't think he's doing it to be distant. I think he's doing it so his hands are free in case he has to fight.

While there has always been tension between the Duvals and the Lockes, there hasn't been outright fighting in a very long time. Longer than I've been alive.

After the fight at the Pack House, I know Bran can hold his own when surrounded by supernaturals, but the Lockes do have quite a few older vampires within their house. Vampires that would nearly match Bran in age and strength.

As we make our way up the curving front steps, I watch him out of the corner of my eye, trying to gauge how he's feeling. This was his idea. But is he worried?

His face is blank.

"We don't have to do this," I whisper beneath my breath.

"Yes, we do," he says evenly just as the double front doors crack open and light spills out.

"Jessie!" A curvy woman comes out of the house with her arms spread for a hug. Maggie is third in line at Locke House and everyone considers her the house's mother.

I let her envelop me and she squeezes just hard enough to make me grunt.

Bran clears his throat and Maggie steps back to give him a look. She clucks her tongue in a tsk-tsk.

"Bran Duval. Good evening. What brings you all the way over here to Locke House?"

While I haven't Pledged yet and certainly haven't aligned myself with the Lockes, I'm still more of a member here than Bran is and I think it might be best if I do most of the talking.

"I need to see Kelly. Where is she?"

Maggie keeps her eyes on Bran and Bran keeps his eyes on Maggie. "I think she's around here somewhere."

"Can you help me find her?"

Maggie tenses up and drags her teeth over her plump bottom lip in a half-wince.

Next to me, Bran goes rigid.

Locke House, like Duval House, is always busy. There are people hanging around in the background and a friendly game of poker going on in the next room over. So I don't notice until several seconds after the vampires that Julian Locke has arrived.

He comes into the square of light cast by the modern chandelier above us. He's wearing a loose-fitting shirt that hides the fact that he's cut like a Greek statue.

His piercing blue gaze sweeps from me to Bran.

"Bran," he says. "Nice of you to visit Locke House. And you brought our girl home." He smiles at me, dares me to contradict him.

I'm not here for conflict so I keep my mouth shut.

But Bran has other ideas.

"Don't provoke me," Bran says. "I know you can smell me on her."

Bran keeps using that fact as leverage against anyone that dares cross the line. I don't want to like it as much as I apparently do. It's a huge turn-on, knowing that every supernatural I cross paths with knows that I'm his.

Gelatin cake.

Gelatin cake.

Julian runs his tongue along the inside of his bottom lip. There's a hint of a disgusted scowl marring his face, but he catches it and widens into a smile instead. "Jessie is free to do as she pleases until her Pledging. If our girl wants to sow some wild oats, so be it."

Now I'm tempted to open my mouth.

Just who does he think he is, disrespecting me like that?

Bran puts his hand out, as if to stop me from jumping Julian. I'm not an idiot, but no one misses that he does it.

"We're just here to speak with Kelly," Bran says. "Can you show us to her?"

Maggie gives Julian a pointed look. The feeling I had with Cody and François comes back, like there's a secret here I'm not supposed to know.

"Maggie?" I say, because I feel more comfortable addressing her than Julian. And also, I trust her more. "Please get Kelly for me. I'm worried about her."

"Oh, don't be!" She squeezes my arm and Bran edges closer to me. "I'll go see if I can find her. How's that sound?"

"Bring her to my office," Julian says. "We'll wait there. Come." He waves us through the foyer. Bran doesn't hesitate and as he follows Julian across the marble floor, he threads his fingers with mine, tugging me close to his side.

I know where Julian's office is—the double doors at the very end of the main foyer hall—but I've never been inside. I've never had a reason to visit him, and I've definitely never been invited.

Once upon a time, when I was maybe thirteen or fourteen, I did have a crush on Julian. It's hard not to. There's something magnetic about him, something quietly intense too.

He's more handsome than gorgeous, more rugged than polished. I think at the time I thought that made him more human than the Duvals.

One look at Bran or Damien and you know they're something other than human.

With Julian, it's a little harder to spot on the first glance.

He opens one side of the double doors on his office and waves us in. The ceilings are soaring, the walls uneven plaster and lathe painted in an off-white paint that contrasts just slightly with the crisp white crown molding.

Bookshelves line the back wall with a marble fireplace in the middle. There's an overstated desk to my left that sits squarely in front of the windows and a sitting area to the right with heavy leather furniture.

"Have a seat," Julian says. "Bran, you want a drink?"

"No."

"Jessie?"

"Um...no thanks."

Julian goes to the bar just inside of the double doors and pours himself a few fingers of vodka. He drinks it straight. Ugh.

"So, Bran," Julian starts.

Bran slowly circles the room, getting extra nosy as he scans the objects in Julian's office. "So, Julian."

"What the fuck are you really doing here? And why are you dragging Jessie into this?"

Bran pauses at a marble bust that sits on one of the shelves. He pulls it off. "Did you know this was a fake?" He turns it over as if inspecting it and then the stone cracks in his grip, raining to the floor in a dozen pieces. "Oops."

Julian's upper lip curls. "You're playing with fire."

Bran dusts off his hands. "No, I'm trying to put one out. One that you started."

Julian's gaze sweeps to me, then he drains the rest of the liquor. "I don't know what you're talking about."

"Don't you?" Bran crosses back to me hovering near the door. "Why don't you tell Jessie why you killed Sasha the night she took Jessie for a ride."

Julian goes eerily still. I don't think he even takes a breath for several long seconds, then, "Sasha left town."

"We know the truth," I hear myself saying. "Please, just tell us the reason."

His nostrils flare with irritation. "Even you know, Duval, that the head vampire of a house can do as he pleases with the vampires bound to his house. It's written in the rules. I don't have to explain myself to either of you."

"That might be the case," I say, "but I'm asking you anyway. Please just tell me what happened."

He screws up his mouth, the glass still clutched in his hand. I swear I hear it crack. "All right. The truth is she bit you that night and so her death was her punishment."

"Even I know that's overkill. No pun intended," Bran says with a smirk.

"I deemed it necessary." Julian returns to the bar and pours a second round. His shirt slouches on his shoulders as he straightens his spine. "Now answer my question. Why the fuck are you toying with Jessie?"

"He's not toying with me," I say and Bran says, "Because I can."

The fuck. I scowl at him with enough venom to singe his eyebrows. If only I really was fae, one of the elementals I've heard about, the ones who can burn a place to the ground with nothing more than a look.

Bran would be tinder by now. Asshole.

Julian frowns at me with open sympathy like I'm just a brainless idiot that got trapped by the big, bad vampire.

"Please don't let him manipulate you any further," Julian says.

"Don't worry about me, okay? This isn't about me."

Or is it?

"I want to see my sister."

Both Bran and Julian's attention wanders beyond the office.

"I think Maggie has her," Bran tells me.

"And?" I coax.

There's a troubling look that comes across Bran's face. And Julian registers it at the same time I do.

The office doors bang open and slam against the wall.

Suddenly I'm alone in the office. "Bran!"

I race out after him. Where the hell did he go?

"Bran!"

I run down the hall and slam into a round table in the middle of the foyer when Kelly's voice causes me to shift directions at the last second.

"What's happening?" Kelly slurs.

I whirl around and see her clutched in Bran's grip, her legs buckling beneath her.

Several higher-ranking Locke vampires are in a loose circle around them.

"Kelly!" I shove in between the vampires to get to my sister's side. I don't see any bites, no trailing blood to explain why she's so pale and dazed.

"Kelly?" I put my hands on either side of her face. She's burning up and slick with sweat. She shakes in my grip. When I force her to look at me, her eyes find mine, bloodshot and glassy.

"Jessie?" Her voice is reedy and thin.

"What's wrong with her?"

Bran adjusts her in his grip. He answers me but looks at

Julian as he does. "It's called compulsion fever. It can happen when a vampire compels a mortal too many times."

The rage that comes over me is nearly blinding.

I don't stop to think about the risks or the consequences.

I don't care about any of that.

I whirl around and charge Julian Locke.

Episode Twenty-Five
Do Not Provoke a Vampire

I was eleven years old when my mother sat me down for The Talk.

Not the birds and the bees.

The vampires and the shifters. The witches and the moons. The magic and the fae.

That's a talk that every mortal child has to have when living in a place like Midnight Harbor. It's a rite of passage.

I can remember being on the playground the winter of fifth grade when Addison Marquor came over to the monkey bars where Sam was dangling from a cold bar and I was eating a sucker beneath her.

Shoulders back and her head held high, Addison proudly told us her mother sat her down at the kitchen table over the weekend and gave her The Talk.

Sam and I were desperate for the details but Addison had always been the type of girl who thought information was gold and anyone who didn't have it was meant to stay poor.

When I finally got to have The Talk, I felt like such an adult. I thought my mom was cracking open the universe and spilling all its secrets.

But it was just a bunch of dumb rules.

Don't go running through Pack territory, especially not close to the full moon when shifter magic is more potent and wolves more volatile.

Do not, under any circumstances, go near the pack alpha under a supermoon.

Don't insult a witch. At least not to her face.

Don't tell the fae "thank you" unless you want to be indebted to them.

Don't walk into a room of vampires and pretend you're anything other than food.

And definitely do not provoke a vampire.

Sorry, Mom. Looks like I'm breaking rules left and right these days.

I go straight for Julian's throat.

I don't have a plan. There is only the one blinding thought: to shred the skin from his bones.

He hurt my sister. He's *supposed* to protect my sister.

As I reach out, teeth gnashed, fingers curled like claws, Julian catches me at the wrists and whirls me around.

Stars blink in my field of vision when he throws me up against the wall and my skull cracks loudly against the plaster.

Suddenly I'm swimming and I can't see straight and a dull ache shoots through my head.

Stupid, Jessie. What were you thinking?!

Julian hoists my arms above my head, just one hand needed to capture my wrists beneath him. His fangs sharpen and his eyes glow bright blue.

"You may not be Pledged to my house—" he starts and then cuts himself off.

Bran is at his back, his eyes like fire, his fangs like razors. "Don't."

"You have no weapon," Julian points out.

"I can tear your heart out through your rib cage."

Julian glances to his right, maybe assessing his chances. There are several vampires inching closer and none of them are on Bran's side.

"If you hurt her," Bran says, his voice low and even, "I will destroy everything you've ever touched."

When Julian turns back to me, his fangs have retracted but the blue glow is still in his eyes. He scans my face, one long sweep of his gaze. "Just a toy, huh?"

Bran says nothing.

The Locke vampires edge closer.

"Bran," I say.

Kelly is slumped in Maggie's arms. Her eyes are drooping like she's high or dying.

I can't leave her here. I can't let Julian have her anymore. I don't know much about compulsion fever, but it looks like it's destroying her from the inside out.

I have to get her out of here.

I give Bran a pleading look. I'm powerless here. And I have nothing to give.

"Let us leave here unharmed," Bran says, "—all three of us," he clarifies. "And I'll give you my lakeside property."

Julian frowns, but he looks over his shoulder. "You think your garish modern house is worth more than—" He cuts himself off and frowns at himself.

"Go on," Bran coaxes. "Worth more than what?"

A door bangs shut somewhere deep in the house and Julian's thoughts wander. His dark brow sinks lower over his flashing blue eyes. Finally, he pulls away from me. "Go on. Take them both if you must. Just blood trash now, aren't they?"

"What did you say?" I yell.

"Mouse," Bran says.

"That was a low blow! He has to—"

"Mouse!" Bran's voice rings with command as he shoots

me a castigating look. Even a few of the Locke vampires shrink back.

I shut my mouth. But inside I'm burning.

Bran scoops up Kelly in his arms and then gestures for me to follow him.

We make it out the door and across the front porch and down the front steps.

At the bottom I look back to the open door to see Julian framed in the golden light of the chandelier behind him, several of his Locke vampires flanking him like soldiers.

Bran might have threatened to destroy Julian, but I'm vowing here and now that when it comes to Julian's demise, it'll be me that wields the wooden stake.

———

Bran drives the Bimmer back to our quiet street. I sit in the back with Kelly's head in my lap, her arms curled into her chest, hands tucked beneath her chin like she's a child.

"I never should have left her after that bite," I say.

With no attention on his speed, Bran gets us across town in less than ten minutes. "Kelly is a big girl, mouse."

"We're all big girls, aren't we? Until we find ourselves in the clutches of a big, bad vampire."

"This isn't a fairytale."

Our houses come into view and I nearly weep at the familiar sight.

"No," I say, as Bran parks in his driveway. "I suppose it's not."

With the engine off, Bran comes around to the backdoor and reaches in for Kelly. She moans, her head lolling, until Bran gets her comfortably in his arms. He makes his way for his front door.

"What are you doing?"

"Julian hasn't been invited inside my house."

"Yeah, but it's owned by a vampire. I thought the magic of the invitation rule only applies to a mortal-owned house."

"I don't own the house," he says.

"Seriously? Who does?"

He doesn't answer me as he turns the door knob and then kicks the door in with the toe of his boot.

There are no lights on inside so I grope around until my eyes adjust to the darkness. I finally locate a light switch and flick it on, and the recessed lighting comes on in the entry hall.

"I'll put her in one of the spare bedrooms," Bran says when he's already halfway up the stairs.

I follow him. It's a three-bedroom house, and Bran picks the first bedroom on the left. There's a queen-sized bed against the wall and two black and white photographs framed in thick black frames that hang above the bed.

I know right away they're Bran's work. I can see his style now that I know what it is. High contrast, interesting subjects, haunting light.

Bran has the duvet pulled back and is depositing Kelly on the bed before I can help.

"What do we do for her?" I ask as I come around and slip off her leather booties. She's wearing her favorite socks, the ones with the pineapples wearing sunglasses. "Is compulsion fever dangerous?"

"Only if you keep doing it." He readjusts the pillow beneath Kelly's head. My heart thuds loudly in my chest seeing him take care of my sister like this.

I hear Julian's words echoing in my head—*just a toy, huh?*

Maybe the reason I didn't lose my mind in Julian's office when Bran insinuated that he was playing with me was because I knew he was bullshitting.

Who was he trying to fool? Julian? Or himself?

"Does she need something while she heals? Like, is there

some old witch's brew that's an antidote? Some ancient elixir? Or—"

"Rest," he tells me with a half-cocked grin on his face. "She'll be okay. I promise. But some pain meds will help break the fever."

"Do you have any?"

He gives me a look like I'm being ridiculous.

"Got it. We have some. I'll run over and get them."

"I'll come with you."

"It'll only take a second."

"Mouse."

"Okay. I guess you're coming with."

Outside, the streetlights cast wide circles of golden light on the pavement. Across the street, the front window on Mrs. Haraway's house is twinkling with golden string lights. She's the neighbor that has her Christmas tree up October to March. And the rest of the year, her house is always decked out in golden string lights.

Further down the block, Mr. Taylor is walking his golden lab.

It's all so normal.

And here I thought I wanted more normal than this.

Instead, I backtracked and descended into the very center of the world of the supernatural.

Even though I've lived in Midnight my entire life, I took this quiet, normal life I had for granted. I wanted to escape it.

Now I just want to come home after a long day working my normal job at the coffee shop and find my sister drinking a glass of wine on the sofa while binge-watching an old season of Real Housewives.

But I don't think I'll ever have that life back.

How could I after the last several days? After everything I've uncovered?

I go to the front door and unlock the deadbolt with my key. I step over the threshold.

I make a big show of turning to Bran and waving out my arm like I'm a showman at a circus. "Bran Duval, won't you please come in?"

He steps inside and comes over to me, wraps his hand around the back of my neck and brings his mouth to my ear. "Good girl," he says, causing a goddamn riot in my panties.

"Damn you," I mutter.

He smirks at me.

We always leave the light on above the stove, so there's a warm glow in the kitchen when I go there for the bottle of ibuprofen.

Bran looks around our living room. It's weird, him being in my space. I've given him more of myself than I've ever given anyone, but seeing him inspect my entire life in the pictures on the wall and the odds and ends on the bookshelves gives me a weird sort of glow. It's almost like he wants to know me better.

I find the pain meds shoved in the back of the vitamin and supplements cabinet.

Bran picks up my monthly copy of *Cosmopolitan*. "Really, mouse?"

There's a bold headline across the bottom that says *The Beginner's Guide to the G-Spot.*

I go over to him and snatch the magazine from his hand. "This is why I didn't want to invite you in."

"More lies." He moves to the built-in cabinets and scans the books on the shelves and pulls out a beloved copy of *Pride and Prejudice*. He holds it up. "Yours or Kelly's?"

"Who do you think?"

"Kelly."

"Yes."

"You're not a romantic at heart," he decides and puts the book back.

He isn't wrong.

"Let me tell you a secret," he says.

"Go on."

"Mr. Darcy was based on my brother."

I burst out laughing. "Really?"

He nods and continues to scan our shelves. "Jane Austen met him at a ball and immediately hated him. And loved him too, I suppose."

I roll my eyes. "Damien seems like the type of guy to be loved and hated. Like his brother, *I suppose.*"

Bran rewards me with another one of those lopsided grins. "We are very much alike, Damien and I."

"Oh really? Does he fuck his neighbor too and call her a toy?"

All of the humor is suddenly gone from Bran's face. "I didn't want Julian to know."

"Know what?"

I can't miss the way Bran's shoulders rise with a heavy breath, the way his chest expands and he closes his eyes.

He's reluctant to answer.

"Know what, Bran?"

"That the thought of him taking you away from me makes me want to murder things."

When he opens his eyes and looks at me, his irises are molten amber.

Warmth spreads through my chest. Of all the answers I thought he'd give me, that wasn't one of them.

I swallow hard and try to catch my breath.

"Really?" I squeak. "Is it because of the sex? Because you like controlling me? Because—"

"No."

"Then wh—"

"If I told you to hide something where you'd never look, where would that be?"

"That's a really weird question."

"Humor me."

I cross my arms over my chest as I think. Somewhere I'd never look? I never go into Kelly's room but I doubt I'd hide something in there. I'd never find it again. There are a few closets in our house that I don't go into often, but I do get an urge to reorganize them at least twice a year.

"Well," I start, "my first guess might be those drawers." I nod at the cabinets. "Kelly loves shoving shit inside of them. Like important documents and stuff so I never have a reason to go in there and if I opened them, and I saw the mess, I'd have to reorganize them and then Kelly would yell at me when she was looking for a thing from nine years ago that she needs *right this second*."

Bran opens one of the drawers in the cabinet and roots around inside.

"What are you looking for?"

He opens the next drawer.

"Bran?"

On the third one, he spots something that makes him pause and then he pulls it out to the light. The envelope has my handwriting on the front. It reads *Important Shit. Don't lose.*

I don't remember writing that. I don't even know what's inside the envelope.

"What is that?" I ask.

Bran is a blur as he crosses the room and comes to a stop in front of me. His speed kicks up a sharp breeze and it sends several loose strands of hair fluttering around my face.

"Open it." He hands it over.

A creeping shiver rolls down my spine. There's this shadow in the back of my mind like I should know this envelope. I should know what's inside.

I finally take it from him with shaking hands. The flap has been sealed, so I run my finger inside the fold and rip it back.

There's a piece of thick, folded paper inside. I pull it out and unfurl it, my fingers rubbing over the embossed symbol of a notary stamp on the bottom.

It's a deed to a house.

The address listed is Bran's house.

And the owner?

Is me.

Episode Twenty-Six

Sin and Regret

"What is this?"

Bran moves around me and starts grabbing things from the kitchen. Bread. Butter. Slices of cheese.

"Bran. Hello?" I go over to him as he dumps everything in a bag. I wave the deed for his house in his face. "What is this?"

He holds out his hand for me to take. I look from it to his face.

"We're going to return to my house—" he says.

"*My* house, apparently."

"—and I'll make you a grilled cheese sandwich, pour you a drink, and tell you everything."

"Where have I heard that before?" I say with a bit more venomous sarcasm than I initially intended.

He doesn't move. Doesn't argue. Doesn't force. Bran Duval knows the art of patience and he knows exactly when to use it.

I huff out a breath and take his hand. He leads me out of the house and across our yards and inside his house. He dumps the ingredients on the kitchen counter, then fills a glass with water from the fridge and hands it to me.

"Go check on Kelly," he tells me. "While I heat up the pan."

I leave him in the kitchen and return to my sister upstairs. She's still sleeping soundly in Bran's spare bedroom despite the glow of the bedside lamp. There's just enough room on the bed beside her so I sit down on the edge and give her a soft nudge. "Kels?"

She stirs and her eyes flutter. "Jessie?"

"Hey."

"Where...*ughhh*." Hand to her forehead, she winces and then kneads at the space between her brows. "Wine headache. What time is it?"

"It's late."

She sits up and looks around. "Where am I?"

"We're at Bran's."

She frowns. "Our *neighbor*? Bran Duval?"

"The one and only."

I can just picture him down in the kitchen being all smug about that.

"Why are we here?"

"It's a really long story." I put my hand to her forehead. She's still hot to the touch. "Here." I shake out two pills and hand her the glass of water. "You have a fever and we need to bring it down."

"What? But—"

"Just trust me. Please take the medicine."

With another wince, she manages to sit upright to down the meds with a swig of water and then collapses back against the pillows. "I'm glad you're here." She smiles sleepily up at me as she drifts off again.

"Me too." I give her hand a squeeze and push the hair from her face. Now that she's with me and I know she's safe, I can feel a phantom knot releasing at the center of me. I hadn't realized until this moment just how important it was to have my sister at my side.

And maybe deep down I always knew she wasn't exactly safe at Julian's side.

When I'm sure Kelly is resting again, I make my way back downstairs. Bran is just tossing a butter-coated slice of bread into a hot cast iron pan. The butter sizzles. Despite the fact that he doesn't eat mortal food, he seems at ease in the kitchen.

I slide onto one of the stools at the counter. "Did you guys have grilled cheese sandwiches back before you were turned?"

"We definitely did not." He lays out two slices of cheese and then covers it with the second slice of buttered bread. "Grilled cheeses weren't mainstream until the 1920s when sliced bread was first invented."

"Is it weird that I feel sorry for you? Because you haven't eaten mortal food since the 1700s? I love food."

"I know you do. And yes, it is weird." He flips the sandwich.

"Grilled cheeses are the best. When the cheese gets all gooey and the bread crusty and—" Something occurs to me. "Hold on. Is that why you call me mouse?"

He glances at me over his shoulder. "I'm shocked it took you so long."

"Honestly, I am too."

A glob of cheese melts from between the slices and pops when it hits the hot pan.

"So," I start. "You were going to purge all of your secrets. How long do I have to wait?"

Bran slides the toasted sandwich onto a plate, then cuts it in half. The bread crunches loudly beneath the bite of the blade.

He puts the plate on the dining room table. "Come sit,

mouse," he tells me and then goes to the bar and pours us each a drink.

I have the distinct impression he's taking extra steps to prepare for this conversation and it leaves an unsettled feeling in my stomach.

I know he's been keeping things from me and I know that even when I demanded his honesty, he was still reluctant to give it. I'd be an idiot to believe otherwise. But I'd be lying if I said it wasn't starting to weigh on me.

Bran sharing his collected information with me would be a sign that he trusts me. And I desperately want it.

I don't think Bran trusts very many people.

But beyond all that, these secrets...they're about me. And I deserve to have them.

I sit and he takes the chair across from me and leans back in it languidly, his tumbler of liquor clutched in his hand.

He looks relaxed. I know he's not.

He waits for me to take a bite.

"If you've never had a grilled cheese, then how do you know how to make them?"

"It's just buttered bread with cheese between it."

But when I take a bite, the bread is the right bit of crunch, the cheese the right bit of melted. I don't know if it tastes better because of the novelty of it being made by a vampire, but it's the best damn grilled cheese I've ever had.

"Mmmm," I say as a string of cheese stretches from my mouth to the sandwich. I break it with my fingers and then eat it like a length of spaghetti.

Bran watches me the entire time with the look of a starving man. He takes a long pull from his drink. "I need you to know something, mouse."

I suck the last of the cheese from my fingertip. "I'm listening."

He takes a deep breath. "There is nothing more valuable in

this world—in *our* world—than secrets. There's always more money to make, but secrets are finite and they always retain their value so long as they remain a secret.

"Kingdoms have fallen because of secrets." He turns his glass on the table, his gaze on it instead of me. "I need you to know that when this began, I wanted the secrets and nothing more."

I hold the sandwich between my hands, suddenly not so hungry. "Okay."

"I need you to know that what this is now"—he gestures between us—"was not what I intended, but now that I—"

He frowns and takes another swig of the liquor and tries again. "I would die for two people in this world—Damien and Jimmy. I thought that would always remain to be true. Two people and no more. But lately, the way I've felt when you... when *someone*—"

I hold my breath.

He sighs and sits forward.

"When someone *what*?"

"If I found you the way we found Kelly?" There's a new heaviness to his expression, a new tightness around his mouth.

"I will do anything for you, mouse. That's what I need you to know." It looks like it pains him to say it. Like he'd rather be admitting anything else.

A lump wedges in my throat. I try to swallow it back, but tears burn in my sinuses, only making the lump bigger.

Is he saying...

Is Bran Duval saying he would die for me?

Tension comes to his jaw again. "I need you to know that how it began and how it is now are not the same."

I give him a quick nod. "Okay. I hear you."

He laughs, low and beneath his breath, takes another swig from the glass. "And now that you know that... I *have* been keeping a great many things from you, mouse. And now it's time I come clean."

———

My stomach churns. I can't eat now. How can I?

I wash down the taste of cheese with a swig of the bourbon. It burns down my throat and warms my belly. I think the alcohol hits my bloodstream immediately because I'm buzzy and hot.

"I'm ready," I say, a little breathless from the booze.

"Are you?"

I nod. "Yes."

"Promise me you won't run."

"I think that depends on what the secrets are."

"I didn't murder anyone."

I laugh nervously. "I guess that's a good sign."

"Promise me, mouse. Because I will chase you and it won't be fun for either of us when I catch you."

The buzziness in my stomach sinks between my thighs and I'm suddenly throbbing.

It might be fun.

I might want to tempt fate.

Bran frowns at me. "*Mouse.*"

"Okay, yes. I promise."

"Do you remember how I told you I bought that lakeside property just to spite Julian?"

"Yes."

"I don't like him. I've never liked him and I like doing things to spite him." He inhales through his nose then gets up to refill his glass. With his back to me, I notice the tension in his shoulder blades, the sweep of bone rising beneath the expensive material of his t-shirt.

"It's been well known in the vampire houses that you were not to be bitten."

"Why? Says who?"

"Julian." Drink poured, he turns back to me. "So to spite him, I bit you." And just so it's clear *when* he means, he adds, "*Last year.*"

I laugh. "No, you didn't."

"Yes, I did."

A creeping chill rolls down my spine. "No, you didn't," I repeat, but I'm less certain this time.

"Your birthday last year," he says and leans against the bar. "You wore a tight summer dress the color of deep forest ivy. You smelled like amber and roses. You looked like sin and regret."

My breathing quickens as my heart kicks up.

"I wanted to devour you the second I saw you. I couldn't explain it then and I still can't explain it now." His eyes flash briefly as his gaze goes distant and his memories return to that night.

It's a tradition in Midnight Harbor to throw a big birthday party the year before your Pledging. It's like your last hurrah before binding yourself to a house. Your year of going out.

I did wear a deep green dress. And the amber-rose scent was a perfume Sam bought me as a present.

All of this is true, but—

"I didn't see you there."

"I know," he says. "I wasn't planning on being there, but Damien and I are partial owners of the Harbor—"

"You are?"

"—and there was an issue with the boiler. Damien sent me because he had other things to attend to and I begrudgingly went."

He takes another sip. "I'll admit, I was in a foul mood.

One, because I had to deal with something as mundane as a boiler and two, because I knew it was your party and the fact that Julian had a moratorium on you annoyed me.

"It was petty. I'll admit that much."

He smiles to himself as he raises his glass again. "I was coming up from the basement and you were stumbling out of the bathroom, drunk. You tripped. I caught you. It was a real cinematic moment, mouse." He drinks. Looks over at me.

My cheeks are burning red.

I don't remember any of this and yet, when he describes it, I sense shadows shifting on the walls, ghosts that I should know the shape of.

"'Bran Duval,' you said to me and laughed. Your lips were swollen like you'd been kissing someone and it immediately made me envious of whoever it was. 'Jessie MacMahon,' I said back and you smiled up at me. 'I like it when you say my name,' you said. 'It sounds hot on your hot face.'"

"Oh god."

He laughs. "You're cute when you're drunk."

"Shut up."

"'You should stop drinking,' I told you. 'Why?' you asked. 'Because of vampires like me,' I'd said. 'Someone might take advantage of you.'"

I have a feeling I know what drunk-me might have said.

"'So why don't you?' you said. 'I'm a tasty snack.'"

Yup. That sounds about right.

"'And you're also drunk,' I pointed out. 'So?'" He shakes his head. "Such a brave little mouse."

His gaze darts back to me, to my mouth. "I kissed you first, bit you second. Not my finest moment," he admits. "Immediately, I could tell there was something off about your blood. I couldn't put my finger on it at the time. It was something nagging me in the back of my head.

"'I'm going to tell everyone I just got bit by Bran Duval on my birthday,' you said to me. I couldn't let that happen. There was the taste of your blood and the smell of the witch amulet around your neck. One odd thing about a mortal girl could be brushed off as a coincidence. Two odd things smelled like a secret." He takes another pull from the glass and sets it down. "I compelled you that night. Made you forget."

Even though I knew that this would be the conclusion to the story, it still pains me to hear it. I think that's the worst part about living amongst vampires. At any moment, they can steal something from your head. Bottle it up and make you forget.

I want to punish him for it, but what would be the point?

"It wasn't long after my birthday party that you moved in next door."

He nods. "You asked me why I left Duval House. That's why. Because I knew there were more secrets to uncover and being closer to you would allow me to get them."

"And? Were there?"

Guilt hardens the sharp lines of his face. "Yes."

I inhale deeply, then chug back the rest of my drink. "Rip it off like a bandage. Go on."

"I started to wonder about your blood. Why it tasted off. You were presented as mortal, living with a mortal family. But Julien was trying to keep you from others. So I started to wonder about your origins. I started digging into your past."

I lick my lips.

"I went to the hospital and looked up your birth certificate."

My breathing quickens. "And?"

The fine lines around his eyes deepen as he frowns at me. "There's no record of you being born in Midnight Harbor."

Episode Twenty-Seven

Full of Ghosts

"That can't be true," I say, but my voice comes out barely a whisper and it's rough, like sandpaper, like it hurts just to get the words out.

"I used a lot of favors to find out otherwise," Bran tells me.

I get up from his dining room table and pace.

Bran is on edge, watching me, ready to chase me if I bolt.

Am I on the verge of running?

Can I run far enough to escape this?

I feel like I've left my body. My feet are moving and my hands are shaking and my heart is beating hard in my chest, but this isn't my life.

It can't possibly be my life.

Just when I think there is an end in sight, another corner comes into view, another turn in the labyrinth.

I look back to Bran when I reach the edge of the living room where the large front window overlooks the darkened street. Before Bran, there were only humans and a few witches that lived in my neighborhood. Not many windows remain lit after midnight.

"If there's no record of me being born, how do you

explain my mom being pregnant? There're pictures of her with her pregnant belly and Kelly standing beside her."

"That does seem to be true." Bran comes over to me. "But she disappeared just a month before her due date. Kelly stayed at Locke House until your mom returned."

I've never once heard Kelly talk about staying with the Locke vampires as a child. How could I have missed that detail? How could Kelly have never mentioned it?

Bran leans his shoulder against the window casing and the glow from the streetlight skims his face in a golden haze.

All of this feels like that, like a waking dream.

All of these secrets.

Him.

Me.

The fact that we've barely spent more than a few hours apart in the last handful of days. The fact that right now, as the ground shifts beneath me again, all I want to do is clutch to him. Fuck him. Lose myself in him.

Somehow, Bran Duval has become the only real thing in my life. The anchor that keeps me rooted to the earth.

He isn't the comforting type, but I can't think of anyone else I'd rather be with right now.

"Do you have a theory about my mom and my birth?" I ask him.

His gaze skips to the street where a cat crosses over the pavement and disappears into the shadows of an evergreen bush.

"I don't have all of the secrets you need," he admits. "There are the facts, though. Your mother disappeared right before you were born. She returned with a baby. Your blood tastes like the fae."

I frown up at him. "I can *lie*. I thought we agreed fae was out?"

He looks back to me. "We did no such thing."

"But—"

"You're forgetting something else, mouse."

I cross my arms. "Okay, what?"

"Once upon a time, we could easily travel between the mortal realm and the fae realm. But not long after you were born, the gate was sealed and all of the fae on this side were stuck here."

"What are you saying?"

"I'm saying, I don't believe in coincidences."

I snort. "Are you trying to tell me that the gate was sealed because of me? Or in relation to me?"

"That's exactly what I'm saying."

"No. That's ridiculous."

"Is it?"

"Yes!" I throw up my arms.

Bran scowls at me like I'm being overly sensitive.

"None of this makes sense." I scrub at my face.

"Have you considered that there's a very simple way of confirming whether or not you're fae? We could have the answer right now if we wanted it."

I go still.

Iron.

It hadn't occurred to me, no. Because I never wanted to believe I could be fae in the first place. And beyond that, iron is hard to come by in Midnight simply for the safety of the fae that do live here. You can't buy iron at the gas station, just like you can't buy a stake or a vial of shifter's bane.

"I don't have any iron sitting ar—"

Bran disappears in a blur, ruffling the hair around my face.

When he comes back and holds out his hand, there's a metal bar strung on a length of leather cord dandling from his grip.

"Shit. I was being sarcastic."

"I wasn't."

"Why do you have that?"

"For the fae, obviously."

"Do you have an entire closet somewhere full of weapons for every creature that lives in Midnight?"

He opens his mouth to answer but I hold up my hand. "Wait. Never mind. I don't want to know."

"Take it from me, mouse," he says.

I tuck my hands beneath my arms.

My heart is suddenly pounding against my eardrums and my mouth is dry.

I don't want to touch it.

Because I don't want to know.

"Mouse."

"Maybe I'll leave Midnight after all," I say eyeing the iron in his hand. "I don't have to do this. No one is making me. Are you going to make me?"

He frowns at me, but it's devoid of his usual edge of irritation.

If I didn't know any better, I'd almost think Bran feels sorry for me.

"You're not leaving," he says.

"If I touch that and—"

"I know."

Tears burn in my sinuses.

I don't want to appear weak in front of Bran, but I'm quickly losing my shit just thinking about the consequences of touching that piece of iron.

If I react to it, that's it.

Then I'll really know I'm fae and my entire life will have been a lie and my mom and sister have been keeping a very big secret from me for who knows what reason.

Bran reaches over and grabs me gently by the wrist. He

guides my hand over his. My fingertips tremble over the bar of iron now lying flat in the palm of his hand.

Is it just me, or can I feel the heat already?

I try to yank my hand back, but you can't fight a vampire's grip and especially not one as old as Bran.

"Please," I say, bordering on a whine.

"Don't you want to know?"

Fuck.

No.

No, I do not.

But I have to know.

I exhale, shoulders deflating.

There's no way to move forward until I do this.

I let Bran lower my hand over his and the second my fingers brush the iron, white hot pain races through my skin.

I yank back with a high-pitched hiss as the pain sinks to bone and reverberates up my arm like someone whacked my funny bone with a baseball bat.

Smoke curls from my hand as a giant red welt blooms across my fingertips.

Tears stream down my face.

Bran tosses the iron aside and yanks me into him, his arms wrapping protectively around me.

Before I can get hold of myself, I'm sobbing into his chest.

Not from the pain.

From the sheer magnitude of the truth.

I cry and cry and cry, body shaking, barely able to catch my breath.

And Bran holds me close, surrounds me with his scent and his protection.

I'm so fucking relieved to have him that I cry harder.

I cry for who I was and who I no longer am.

I cry for the void at the center of me, where so many unknowns still lurk.

When the tears finally dry up and I can take a full breath without it catching on a sob, Bran blurs away and returns with a tissue.

I plop onto the couch and dry my face and tuck my hair behind my ears.

Am I surprised by this?

This isn't new information, only a confirmation.

It could be worse. I could have found out I was an honest-to-god mouse shifter.

Bran hands me my glass of liquor. I take a generous sip and let the alcohol warm my insides and drive away the tension building at my breastbone.

Everything is going to be okay.

I'm going to be fine.

I've got this. I can handle this. I can—

Bran looks over me at the stairs.

"What?" I ask.

"It's Kelly," he says. "She's up."

———

We wait for her to come downstairs on her own. It takes her a good twenty minutes and I pace the entire time.

When her footsteps finally hit the staircase, I hurry over to the bottom and peer up at her as she descends. Her eyes are heavy and circled in shadows, but some of the color has returned to her cheeks and she doesn't shine with sweat anymore.

"Jessie?" she says when she sees me standing beside Bran. "What is going on?"

"You had compulsion fever," I explain. "We brought you here to keep you safe."

She comes down the last few steps, her hand trailing on the banister. The black nail polish on her fingernails has started to chip away. Kelly never goes longer than a week without getting her nails done.

"Keep me safe from who?"

"Julian," Bran answers.

Kelly rakes her teeth over her bottom lip. The look she gives me next is haunted and hollow. It's the look of someone who knows they've been drowning.

Why didn't she tell me she was in trouble? We could have figured it out together.

"Kelly, I really, *really* need you to tell me everything," I say. "I know you've been keeping things from me. I can't take the mystery anymore."

My sister frowns at me and her gaze goes distant. "I..." She licks her lips and closes her eyes. "I don't know if I can."

"Why not?"

She leans her weight into the column at the base of the staircase banister. "It's...when I try..." She squints as if trying to make out the shape of the secrets from a distance.

"She's been compelled to forget," Bran says.

I go to my sister's side. "Try harder, Kels."

Her eyes turn watery as she taps at her forehead. "It's all a blank right here. And my head is still pounding and..." She trails off again. "Wait."

"What?"

"Mom!" Kelly clutches at my hand and squeezes. "Mom wrote you a letter. Julian didn't know about it so he couldn't compel me to forget."

"Where is this letter?" Bran asks.

"At the house. In our mother's bedroom."

"Come on." Bran darts for the door and yanks it open. "We'll go together."

———

When Mom died, after we picked out a funeral outfit, Kelly and I shut her bedroom door and pretty much sealed it off.

I've been in there twice since then and every time I get the creeps like I'm walking into a tomb.

As we step over the threshold now and Kelly flicks on the bedside lamp, a shiver crawls down my spine.

Mom's hairbrush is still on the dresser. Her earrings from when she last took them off rest beside the brush. The romantic comedy she was reading sits on the bedside table, her favorite bookmark still tucked inside the pages where she left off.

The bed is made, but it's full of ghosts.

The room still smells faintly of her perfume. The sweetness of jasmine and clary sage and vanilla.

It only takes one deep breath of the scent to immediately transport me to a time when Mom was alive and her life filled this room.

It makes me miss her all over again.

"Where's this letter?" Bran asks.

"Um..." Kelly turns a circle in the center of the room. "It's..." She goes to the dresser and pulls open the bottom drawer, then shoves aside several folded sweaters. "Here."

She hands me an envelope with my name written across the front.

Just hours ago, I was taking a different envelope, tearing open its flap, unraveling its secrets.

That envelope produced a deed to a house.

What will this one give me?

I look up at Bran and Kelly, both watching me with barely constrained apprehension.

Unlike Bran's envelope, this one isn't sealed, but the flap is tucked inside.

I find a letter folded up and my mother's looping cursive scrawled across the paper.

I read it out loud.

Dear Jessie,

If you're reading this, it means I'm not there to tell you myself and that absolutely breaks my heart. I hope your sister is by your side. If she is, I know she's doing the very best she can under the circumstances. Please go easy on her.

First, I need to tell you, everything I did I did with a mother's love.

After your father died, and after I somehow managed to crawl out of the grief to the extent I could function, I was so grateful to be pregnant with his baby. I could have one more piece of him by my side.

But then the absolute worst thing happened—I started having complications.

After many tests and several visits to the doctor, I found out the baby was dying. I petitioned Julian and asked for his blood, but he refused. Vampire blood while a baby is in gestation can result in Very Bad Things.

Yes, all caps. That's the impression I got when he explained it to me.

I went to Rita next and she performed a healing spell but it didn't take.

I had one last idea. One last ditch effort.

I was so desperate to save a piece of your father.

So I went to the faerie realm and sought out fae magic.

But by the time I found someone willing to help, I was already in labor. I passed out, the pain was so intense, and when I woke, there was a baby in my arms.

You smiled up at me and when you cooed, I swear my heart swelled in size.

I loved you so much.

Instantly. Without question.

When I returned with you to Midnight, I thought we'd been blessed with a miracle.

But then...strange things started happening.

And I started to doubt that the baby I had in my belly when I went to the fae realm was the baby that I returned with.

You were just over a year old when I took you for a walk through the park and we crossed paths with a fae, a brownie.

He immediately came over to us and got down on one knee in front of you and peered at you like he was inspecting a strange creature. He said to me, "Did you steal her?"

"She's my daughter," I told him.

"What you believe and what is true are not the same thing."

And then he walked away like he hadn't just shattered my entire world.

Because deep down, I knew, I *knew* you weren't my flesh and blood.

Right then and there, I had to make a decision.

The fae realm had already been sealed off by this point, so I had nowhere to go, no one to turn to.

I went to Rita begging for help again, but I couldn't tell her what you were. I was too afraid of what others would do if they found out the truth. Like the brownie, I worried they would think I kidnapped you and the fae, while peaceful here, have never exactly been on our side.

I asked for a binding spell and Rita performed it, no questions asked.

I did it to protect you and if I'm honest, to protect me and your sister too.

The things you did, Jessie...you were only a year old and it *terrified* me.

If you're reading this, I'm begging you, burn it and forget about it and go on with your life.

Sometimes, baby girl, secrets are better left buried.

EPISODE TWENTY-EIGHT

LOUDLY AND WITHOUT RESTRAINT

TERRIFIED.

That was the word my mother used to describe the strange things happening around me before I was bound by Rita's magic.

When I was only a year old.

What. The. Hell.

When I look up at Bran, the expression on his face makes me a little ill.

There's the barest glimpse of fear pinched in the fine lines around his eyes.

Then it's gone, tucked away.

Bran Duval cannot afford to be afraid.

Even of little mice.

Kelly comes over to me and wraps me in a hug. We're nearly the same height, so I get a face full of her hair. It doesn't smell like her expensive shampoo though. It smells like Locke House, like vodka and cigar smoke.

She cries against me. "If I knew...I mean, maybe I did and Julian made me forget. But you're...we'll always be sisters no matter what."

"Of course we will." I squeeze her tightly. Do I feel different knowing she's not my blood sister? Do I even want to believe it's true?

There's a little voice in the back of my head that says subconsciously I always knew.

Maybe that was why I was so desperate to leave Midnight. I didn't feel like I fit in my own skin, let alone the life I thought I was destined for.

"I'm so sorry, Jess," Kelly says to me. "I'm so, so sorry."

"It's okay."

"No, it's not," Bran says.

Kelly pulls away and frowns at him. "Excuse me. I don't need—"

I squeeze my sister's arm. "He's just like that. You'll get used to it."

"Why would I have to?" She frowns at me.

"Because he isn't going anywhere," I say. "You were the one who wanted Duval House to bid on me, anyway."

"I—*right*." She presses at the space between her brows. "I forgot about that. Your Pledge is..."

"Technically tomorrow, now that it's after midnight."

"Tomorrow? Oh fuck. I haven't planned the party! What are we—"

"I think we have more important things to worry about." I give the letter in my hand a shake.

"We still need a party! Your Pledge will happen, letter or not. I need a glass of wine and my planner. I need to start making a to-do list."

"Slow down, Kels."

"We need a party!" she shouts.

"Okay. I know. We'll have a party."

The outburst catches me by surprise and I just stare at her as she stares at me, eyes wide. This is so unlike her. Both of us are the non-confrontational sort. Sometimes to our detriment.

We'll often leave things unsaid when really, we should be communicating them, even if it's hard.

Kelly exhales and folds her arms over her middle. "You deserve a celebration."

"While I am positively thrilled about planning a party," Bran says, which gets a scowl out of me because I know he's being sarcastic, "we have an issue we should discuss right now. Julian might have let us leave his house, but he'll be looking for another way to get what he wants. Namely you, mouse."

"Mouse?" Kelly frowns at me.

"Long story."

"Because you like grilled cheese so much." She laughs to herself. "Clever."

"I am a clever boy," Bran says, still dripping with sarcasm.

I had no idea what I was getting into, putting Bran and my sister in the same room. I don't know if I like it.

"What do you propose we do about Julian?" I ask him.

"He'll continue to use Kelly against you. She's pledged to his house, so he'll have some strings he can pull to get her back."

Kelly deflates. I slide my arm over her shoulders. "There must be something we can do."

"We can petition the court to reverse her pledge," Bran says.

"We can?"

Kelly nods. "Yes. Technically that's true, but they're rarely approved."

"That's because they rarely have the backing of a Duval."

Kelly gives him a look. "The arrogance of a Duval is simply astounding."

"It's not arrogance if it's fact."

"We petition the courts. What do we say?"

"*I* petition the court," Bran says. "I will attest to finding Kelly with compulsion fever. On its own, it's not necessarily a reason to reverse a pledge, but if I'm asking for it, it'll go through."

"And then what?" Kelly asks. "I'll be without a house. Without protection. Julian won't let it go that easily."

"That's true. Which is why you'll be adopted by Duval House."

Kelly snorts. "You must be joking."

"He doesn't joke," I say. But also, seriously? "What will Damien say?"

"Damien and Kelly used to fuck before she was Pledged to Locke House. So I doubt he'll object."

"Excuse me!" Kelly shouts.

I cut a look to my sister. "You slept with Damien Duval and didn't tell me?!"

Kelly is still shooting daggers at Bran when she says to me, "It was a very long time ago."

"Was it?" Bran challenges, like he already knows exactly how long ago it was.

"I can't believe you didn't tell me," I say.

"It was...it wasn't something I wanted to go around shouting from the rooftops, okay? I wasn't in a good place."

"Not a good place? If Damien is anything like his brother, I'd say it was probably fucking nirvana."

"Jessie!" She whacks me on the arm.

"What?" I laugh and rub at the sting as it fades. "I'm proud of you, is what I'm saying. You're not usually the scandalous type."

"I'm not!"

"Was it good?" I whisper behind the cup of my hand, like Bran can't hear me. "Is Damien amazing in bed?"

"Mouse," Bran says in his scolding tone of voice.

When I look across the room at him, his eyes are starting to fire. "I suggest you stop asking about how good my brother is in bed."

There's considerable tension in the lines around his mouth. Is he jealous? We've yet to have a discussion about what this actually is between us. Vampires don't put girl-friend/boyfriend labels on their relationships usually, but are we *in* a relationship? Are we exclusive? Am I overthinking this?

When the glow in his irises intensifies, an errant thrill buzzes between my legs. My heart thumps harder. Bran's chest expands as he takes in a deep breath.

"Mouse."

I straighten. "Okay. I hear you."

"Wait." Kelly frowns. "Are you saying you're sleeping with *him*?"

I make an innocent face at her. "Maybe?"

"Jessie!"

"I'm growing less and less fond of this conversation as it goes on," Bran says.

"Is he fond of anything?" Kelly asks.

Mmmmm, yes. Teasing the living daylights out of me with his clever fingers and dirty mouth.

The buzz comes back and Bran scowls at me.

"Okay, so when do we petition the courts?" I ask, trying to shift the night back to the business at hand.

"Now," Bran says.

"Now?" Kelly squeaks.

"Is there a better time? The vampire courts are only open at night." He tilts his head, pinning her with a look. "Or perhaps we give Julian a few days to plot his revenge?"

Kelly plops onto the edge of Mom's bed. The frame creaks. "Will Damien...I mean...have you spoken to him about this?"

"I have, yes," Bran says.

I can't ignore the way Kelly flushes, talking about Damien.

I had no idea. How did I miss that? I guess I've always been a little oblivious to my sister's personal life.

"What did he say?" A thread of hope turns her voice thin.

"He agreed to it."

There's a faint smile tugging at the corner of my sister's lips before she brings her hands in front of her face, hiding it.

Maybe like me, my sister saw her life going in an entirely different direction.

Maybe like me, she's spinning, unsure of where she'll land but is hopeful that it'll be better than where she started.

"Until we get an approval from the court, you'll stay at my house," Bran says.

"*My* house," I correct.

The look he gives me is akin to the smack of his hand across my ass. And thinking about it, my clit throbs, new wetness soaking my panties.

I have to stop thinking about Bran doing naughty things to me or we'll never get through the night.

"I'll pack a bag," Kelly says and leaves us.

I go across the hall to my room and Bran follows me. A chill creeps down my spine. If I thought him being in my living room was bad, my bedroom will be far worse.

Did I clean my room last I was here? I mean, I always have a clean room but what if I left something out that I don't want him to see?

I quickly scan the dresser, the desk, the bedside table. My room is neat and uncluttered, but I spot a stupid picture of Sam and me from last summer where we're making funny faces at the camera.

I snatch it from the mirror hanging above my dresser and quickly shove it into my top drawer.

"How long do you think we'll be staying at your house?" I ask as I head into the closet.

Bran doesn't immediately answer me and when I turn

around, he's suddenly there. He presses into me and I bang against the door. "If you don't get control of yourself, little mouse," he says, "I'll take you right here, right now. I'll fuck you loudly and without restraint." He takes my wrist in hand and brings my arm up, baring the pale underside. He traces a vein with the tip of his finger, sending a warm jolt down my belly and gooseflesh down to my elbow.

"Maybe *you* should control *yourself*," I argue.

"Oh, should I?" Fangs protrude from his mouth.

"Yes."

"But you're so tempting." His eyes go vampire bright in the dimly lit closet, and then he sinks his fangs into my wrist.

It's unexpected and I gasp, instinct telling me to pull away. But Bran holds fast to me, one hand on my wrist, the other snaking to the back of my neck.

There is an immediate primal need to go still beneath the pressure as he sucks the blood from my veins. Within seconds, I'm drenched.

Behind closed lids, the world sways as the air in my lungs stutters up my throat.

I want him to take me. Right here. Right now. *Loudly and without restraint.*

There's a sudden chill at my wrist when Bran's mouth leaves me.

I whimper at the absence of his warmth.

With the swipe of his thumb, he catches a rogue drop of blood from the corner of his mouth and sucks it back. His eyes are still glowing as he watches me.

"A word of caution, mouse," he says.

I pant against the door, wound up tight. "What?"

"Don't talk about other men in bed." His leans in again and slips his hand inside the waistband of my pants, sending a flash of heat down to my core.

"Or what?"

"Or I'll lose my fucking mind."

His fingers trail along the seam of my panties.

"If talking about other men in bed gets you like this, maybe I don't want to stop."

The rumble of laughter deep in his chest is almost sinister. "You have no idea what you're getting yourself into."

"You're probably right."

On my next breath, he invades my panties and roughly shoves two fingers inside of me. I gasp out as he grabs me around the throat, forcing my chin up, exposing the column of my neck to his fangs.

"I'm going to spend every waking minute making sure everyone knows you're mine." Then he sinks those fangs into my throat.

Episode Twenty-Nine
Vampire Boyfriend

Delirium is a state of mind characterized by restlessness and incoherence.

Pressed against my open closet door, when Bran fucks me with his fingers and drinks the blood from my neck, I think I sink into delirium.

And what a place it is.

Every thrust of his fingers is rough and punishing, and the force of it has the closet door banging against the wall behind me and my heart banging against my ribs.

Being with Bran like this always feels like a leap off a suspension bridge.

Illicit and a little reckless.

When his teeth leave my throat and he towers over me, blood drips from one of his fangs. I'm in a V-neck, so when the blood lands on me, it trails down the valley of my cleavage.

Bran ducks down and runs his tongue from the swell of my breast all the way up the crimson line, sending a full-body shiver straight to my core.

When he straightens again and hangs his head back, eyes

heavy, lost in the ecstasy of the taste of my blood, I can't help but marvel at the sight of him.

Like he's walked out of some macabre renaissance painting, all hard lines and pale, sharp beauty.

Some days, I don't know what to do with him and I'm terrified that I can't contain him, his thirst, his violence, the rawness of the power that runs through his veins.

Some days I'm worried that he'll wake up one evening and realize he's too much for me too.

"What is it?" he asks, his voice thick with bloodlust.

"What are we?"

The question is out before I can gnash my teeth to trap it. I thought it, but I didn't mean to ask it.

I don't want to know what he thinks we are in case it's different than what I think it is.

He still has two fingers inside of me and he rubs his thumb over my clit as he slowly withdraws, then slides back in.

I collapse against the door, weak and trembling.

"Labels are just a way to persuade someone to act or be a certain way." He slides in slowly again, presses his thumb against me. The wave is building, a slow, steady build.

"That's a bullshit answer," I say a little breathless.

"You want me to say you're my girlfriend?" He pushes in hard. It catches me off guard and I yip as the door bangs against the wall again. "You want me to tell everyone I'm your boyfriend?" He puts pressure on my clit, holds it there.

I wiggle beneath him but he's unshakeable. The delirium crawls up my throat, the restlessness up my bones. I want to scream.

"Maybe," I say.

"Are you still leaving Midnight?"

His thumb moves, just barely a flicker and the sensation sends a jolt of pleasure through me, goosebumps down my arms.

I'm *this* close. My nerves are clawing for release.

"I don't know." I'm just baiting him now and he catches on easily enough.

His fingers pull out of me and I moan at the loss of him.

"Try that answer again," he says.

I swallow hard. I've never been bold. Not until I got myself entangled with Bran. It's a little liberating, saying and doing whatever the fuck you want.

"I want to stay," I admit. "With you. I want to stay *with* you."

He props his hand above me and leans in, bloody and still a little sharp with hunger and lust.

"And I don't want this"—I grab the considerable bulge between his legs and he groans—"inside anyone else."

He breathes out through his nose. "The little mouse has finally found her voice, has she? What if I say no?"

Now he's baiting me.

And even though I agreed to obey him, I'm not about to roll over and be a doormat.

"If you get to fuck whoever you want, then so do I."

His eyes tighten, fine lines fanning out as the very thought sends him spiraling into prickly rage. "Absolutely not."

I know what I'm asking him is pretty much unprecedented. Even when he was with Sky, he was sleeping with other women. He's never had a blood mate. Or at least not since I've been alive. I also know women throw themselves at him.

How could they not? Look at him.

But I'm not going to be some side piece.

The thought of him with someone else makes me want to smash things.

"Then tell me what we are," I challenge.

He frowns down at me. "I will not be a vampire

boyfriend." He says *boyfriend* like what he really meant to say was *terrorist* or *hobo*.

"I don't care what you call it so long as we both abide by the same set of rules."

The air grows charged between us. He leans in closer, his mouth just inches away from mine. "I would murder anyone who touched you."

I think he might actually mean it this time.

"Do you know how many men I've murdered over a girl?"

"No."

"None." He brings his hand to my jaw, rubbing his thumb over my bottom lip. "If that's not loyalty, mouse, I don't know what is."

"Say it," I press as he leans closer, my heart raging in my chest. "Tell me."

He rips off my pants, then my panties and lifts me easily. It's hard not to feel small and fragile in the arms of a vampire and I pant out an excited breath.

"I will never"—I hear the familiar rasp of a zipper—"feel another pussy wrapped around my cock for as long as you live. I swear it on my life."

He positions the head of his cock at my opening and I get a buzzy thrill at the thought of him being mine, followed immediately by a seed of doubt. He'll be a twenty-something vampire forever. I can't imagine being sixty years old someday, gray and wrinkly, the promise still lingering between us.

That is until I remember I'm fae.

Fae stay young for a very, very long time.

He pushes in an inch. I'm so wet, so eager for him that he has to hold himself steady so he doesn't slip further.

"Will that suffice, little mouse?" His mouth brushes against mine, featherlight.

I pant out, my breath hot between us. "I think so."

"Try again," he scolds and shoves in further. I sense him

straining against me, desperate to fill me up. His patience must be legendary. I don't know how he's holding back.

"Yes." I nod for emphasis, just as desperate to feel the full length of him.

"Good." He thrusts in. The door bangs. I tighten my grip around his neck.

Bran Duval always keeps his promises.

He fucks me loudly and without restraint.

————

Even though I changed into a nice dress and brushed out my hair, when I come downstairs and find my sister on a stool at the kitchen island, I can't help but feel like I'm doing a walk of shame. My face pinks when she gives me a look like I'm being irresponsible and ridiculous.

"Was that really necessary?" she asks me.

"Yes," Bran answers.

Kelly frowns at him. I'm reminded of her calling him a boy when he first moved in next door. Kelly looks a handful of years older than Bran and I think sometimes she fixates on that to make herself feel better.

Damien looks closer to her age in human years.

"I don't know if I like you having your way with my sister," Kelly says.

Bran gives her a blank look. "I don't really care what you like."

"Hey. Both of you. I'm standing right here."

Kelly sighs. There's a glass of wine in her left hand, the glass only half full.

"We should go," Bran says. "Monday mornings at the courts are always busy."

"Oh, you mean the notorious Bran Duval doesn't have a skip-the-line card?" Kelly quips.

"Depends on who's manning the line." Like a magician pulling a tablecloth from beneath a dinner set, Bran snatches the wine glass from my sister's hand. One second, she's tipping it back and the next it's just gone from her grip. She doesn't realize it until she opens her mouth to drink and there's nothing there.

"Hey!"

"You can't petition while drunk. It's against the law."

She huffs out a breath. Kelly works for the human courts. She knows the rules and can't argue with facts.

"We'll pick you up a fresh bottle on the way home," I say, trying to smooth things over and make her feel better. I think I'm realizing she's been dealing with far more than she's let on. The wine was just to numb herself.

This entire time, I've been blaming her. I was the victim, she was the perpetrator hiding things from me, keeping secrets.

But Kelly was just trying to hold us together and doing the very best she could.

"Depending on what the court says, perhaps we could go to Duval House afterward," Bran amends. "You can select a vintage from our wine cellar. I have several bottles of a 1985 red from Château Mouton Rothschild in France. It's nearing the end of its peak and needs to be uncorked soon."

Bran has wine older than me.

Sensing the olive branch, Kelly softens. "Okay. That sounds amazing, actually."

He nods at her, then makes his way for the door. "Come, MacMahon sisters. Before the night gets away from us."

It's hard to ignore the command of a Duval.

Clearly my sister already knows this because she gets up without question and follows Bran out the door.

———

The drive to the courthouse takes all of six minutes with Bran behind the wheel. I'm full of butterflies the entire way. Not because of the speed, but because Kelly and I are clearly embarking on something that will change both our lives.

The entire town will be talking about this by dinnertime tomorrow.

And I can only imagine how Julian will take the news.

I just hope everything works out for my sister.

I don't want to see her hurting again.

I'm not sure what went on between her and Damien and I have to admit, I'm a little worried about her future in Duval House because of it.

Damien, like Bran, has never had a blood mate, but he's had plenty of women and being Head of House only attracts more. I don't want to see my sister get tangled up with that. In a way, as the head of one of the most influential houses in Midnight, Damien is a king and kings always tend to destroy what they touch.

Maybe he's moved on. Maybe my sister has too.

But when we walk up to the grand front entrance to the vampire court, Damien Duval is there waiting for us.

Episode Thirty
Willful Misconduct

"What is he doing here?" I whisper to Bran.

"*He* can hear you," Damien calls across the parking lot.

I wince. You'd think I'd know better having grown up in a town of vampires.

Bran doesn't say anything, but I get the feeling he doesn't really know either.

The vampire courthouse, situated on the north end of downtown Midnight, sits directly across from Kramwell Park. The park sprawls over several acres of rolling land with a large pond in the center, a paved biking trail that winds around it, and a little café along the edge.

Even though it's well after midnight, the park is full of life. The café, constructed to look like a 19th century conservatory done entirely in glass, glows like a snow globe in the night.

When Mom was alive, we'd pack food in a vintage picnic basket and come to the park in the summertime to sit on one of the gently sloping hills.

Kelly and I haven't done it since Mom died and I feel a pang of sadness at the thought of it now.

We cross the parking lot beneath the soft light of the old-fashioned streetlamps and Damien waits for us, leaning against the stone building like a dark vision.

He's wearing all black just like his brother and from afar, when they're standing next to each other, you could easily mistake them for twins.

But Damien's hair is shorter, his lips thinner, and his gaze a little more penetrating.

"Kelly," Damien says, his eyes sweeping over her, not in a hungry way, more like he's checking her for wounds.

"Hey," my sister answers. "Hi."

They stare at each other for an eternity.

Bran says something in a language I don't speak. I think it's French.

Damien's eyes tighten and he responds the same way.

"You know, it's rude to talk in another language in front of people who don't speak the language."

Damien's tense gaze settles on me, but when he speaks, it's still in French.

Bran grits his teeth and says something low and below his breath.

Kelly, always wanting to unravel confrontation, looks at Damien. "Are you sure you're okay with this?"

"Of course." He acts like he wants to reach out to her but clasps his hands behind his back instead. "Julian has overstepped. He must be held accountable."

And also the Duval brothers hate Julian, so I think this is really a win-win for them.

I remember one of my first conversations with Bran when he told me Kelly promised Damien something he'd been wanting for a very long time if he bid on me.

Now I'm desperate to know what that is. My sister? Power over Julian? Revenge against Julian?

I don't know where their war began. Jimmy insisted most vampire feuds start over lovers and cattle.

Were Julian and Damien fighting over my sister?

"And if it's approved?" I ask Damien. "If the courts allow my sister to leave Locke House, can she be adopted by Duval House? She won't be safe otherwise."

Kelly avoids looking at Damien. I think she's just as worried about her life after this as I am. But maybe for different reasons.

"I don't much care what the court says," Damien answers. "Kelly will come home with me."

My sister's eyes dart to the older Duval brother as her cheeks pink beneath her freckles. I quickly reach over and take her hand in mine and squeeze. Her grip is clammy but tight, like she's holding on for dear life.

I don't blame her.

Since I've become involved with a Duval, every day feels like a hurricane.

"Shall we?" Damien gestures to the front entrance.

Bran shifts in front of me and pulls one of the doors open. They're easily ten feet tall and made of solid wood with windows inlaid with an iron diamond grid. The door creaks and clanks the way I think a door would on a medieval castle.

The vampires like their drama. Even their entrances are dramatic.

Inside, iron lanterns hang from the tall ceiling and intricately carved metal sconces flicker golden on the wood paneled walls.

Bran leads the way, but Damien stays at our back, sandwiching us between two Duvals. I can't help but shiver.

We go down the main hall, then cut left down another where a sign hangs from the wall and reads *Small Claims Court*.

But there's nothing small about this.

I'm aware that something of this magnitude will shake up Midnight Harbor. The Duvals are never involved in this sort of thing. No mortal has ever been important enough to start a potential war.

I look over at Kelly. Her face is blank, but her hand is shaking in mine.

We enter into a clerk office. There are seven people in line ahead of us but Bran clears his throat and the others scatter like dry leaves on pavement.

He goes to the head of the line and the woman sputters. "Good morning, Mr. Duval. What can I do for you?"

"Pledge petition."

"Oh?" Her eyebrows rise. "Oh. Okay. Sure." She rifles through some papers and produces a single application that she sticks beneath the metal arm of a clipboard. "This needs to be filled out and turned in before you can go before the council."

Bran takes the clipboard and a pen and returns to us. There's a bank of waiting room chairs against the wall, so Kelly and I sit. Bran and Damien remain standing and Bran fills out the form, his hand a blur across the paper.

He frowns at a line, looks up at Damien, and asks him something in French.

Damien gives him a quick response.

Within minutes, the form is complete and Bran returns it to the woman.

We don't wait long. I guess whoever is manning the line today is the right person to move us ahead.

I can vaguely recall a study unit in my government class in high school that covered the supernatural courts. Each supernatural—vampire, shifter, and witch—get their own court, but a representative from the other factions serves on each council. The fae don't have a court, unfortunately. They never saw a reason to start one, since they had always gone back and forth between the realms and they had their own system on the fae side.

I wonder if those stuck here are regretting that decision now. They literally have no representation.

When we walk into the courtroom, we're ushered in front of a bench where two vampires sit next to a shifter and...

"Bianca?" I blurt.

I went to school with Bianca, though she was a few years ahead of me. She's one of the witches from the Mulligan family. I had no idea she was a councilwoman now.

She's wearing a tailored black blazer with a high collar that stands around her long, pale neck almost like armor. Her short blond hair is cut in a sharp bob. It's tucked behind her left ear where a diamond encrusted cuff glitters on her lobe.

I shouldn't be surprised she's here. She was always ambitious, incredibly smart, and heavily into politics. She was class president in junior high and high school and often volunteered during local elections. She loves this kind of thing.

"Hi Jessie," she says and then her gaze sweeps over the Duvals and she gives me a frown.

I want to explain to her. I want her to know that I know what I'm doing (do I?) but one of the vampires on the bench starts speaking and I clamp my mouth shut again.

"Case Number 0788358," the vampire says, his voice booming across the room. "Duval vs. Locke. Pledge petition for one—" He scans the form. "Kelly MacMahon?"

"That's correct, *Vasill*," Damien answers.

I remember *vasill* from my class. The title is the vampire equivalent for a judge.

"What's the charge?" the *vasill* asks.

"Willful misconduct," Damien answers. "My brother, Bran, and Miss MacMahon, Kelly's younger sister, found Kelly suffering from compulsion fever earlier in the night. In addition to that, several nights ago, Kelly also returned to her mortal home with a sizeable neck wound." Damien stops and his jaw flexes, teeth gritting.

After a deep breath, he adds, "Ms. MacMahon was healed only by the blood of my brother. I would like to petition for permanent adoption of Ms. MacMahon, as is my right by vampire law."

Bianca's eyes widen.

"We can't approve a legal adoption of a pledge until we've allowed Julian Locke to speak in his defense," the *vasill* points out.

"Yes, but you can approve a temporary removal order for the safety of the pledge as is stated in Section 71.329 of the Pledge Civil Rights Act."

My head is literally spinning with all of the legal speak. I'm suddenly grateful Damien is here. I think he had all of this planned out before he took one step into the courthouse.

He knew he wanted to win today and he knew just how to do it.

"I have a question for the MacMahon sisters," Bianca says.

Kelly and I, hands still linked, step forward.

"First, do you have any objection to the Duvals adopting you into their house?"

Beside me, Kelly shakes her head, then clears her throat. "No, councilwoman."

Bianca folds her hands on the bench and her shoulders scrunch up, causing the collar of her blazer to stand further erect around her face. "And do you know what you're doing? Right now?" She narrows her eyes, assessing. "Do you understand what you're asking for?"

Yes. No. Maybe? *Do we, Kelly?*

Maybe Kelly and I are both in over our heads. It's all fun and games fucking Bran, being with Bran, but what happens after tomorrow? What happens if Kelly is adopted into Duval house?

Where do I go for my pledge?

I look over at my sister, at the exhaustion smudged

beneath her eyes, the downturned corners of her mouth, the paleness of her skin.

We have so much left to figure out, but I want her by my side. She may not be blood, but she is my sister and she's the only family I have left.

"We do, councilwoman," I answer. "My sister's safety is my highest priority."

Kelly smiles at me. She pats our linked hands, then kisses me on the cheek. "My answer is the same as my sister's. I'll do anything for her and Julian Locke is..." Her voice catches. I catch the glint of tears welling in her eyes.

"He's what?" Bianca prompts.

"He's—"

The courtroom door slams open.

We all turn to the commotion.

Julian Locke is there, a piece of paper clutched in his hand. "Stop!" he shouts. "Kelly MacMahon cannot be adopted into Duval House."

"Mr. Locke," the *vasill* says, "you'll be given ample opportunity to def—"

"She can't be adopted into Duval House," he says again. "Because she's my blood mate." He waves the piece of paper in his hand. "And I have the signed license right here to prove it."

EPISODE THIRTY-ONE
SOMETHING DARK STIRRED

MY SISTER IS JULIAN LOCKE'S BLOOD MATE? THAT can't be right.

"Approach the bench, Mr. Locke," the *vasill* instructs and Julian walks passed us to the front of the courtroom.

He looks over his shoulder at Damien for the briefest of seconds and I swear I catch a flicker of triumph on his face.

That mother fucker.

The *vasill* takes the blood mate license from Julian and reads it over. "Ms. MacMahon," he says, "did you perform the blood mate ceremony and sign this license?"

My sister sputters beside me. "I...that's not...*no*, your honor. I wouldn't—" She looks at Damien. Her breathing is labored and her eyes wide. "I wouldn't," she says low and beneath her breath.

When he meets her eyes, Damien's expression is blank, but his hands are fists at his side.

The *vasill* hands the license to one of the courtroom guards. "Take that to Ms. MacMahon please."

The guard, another vampire, brings it over and holds it up for all of us to see.

"Is that your signature, Ms. MacMahon?" the *vasill* asks.

"Fuck," Kelly whispers.

It is her signature. My sister has very distinct handwriting. It's half print, half cursive, with tall, skinny letters.

Her K dips down far on the signature line and her Y loops with a curl on its tail.

"As you can see," Julian says, "as my blood mate, Kelly MacMahon should be returned to me and this matter resolved immediately."

"Even a blood mate has rights," I blurt.

The guard hands the license back to Julian. I want that piece of paper so I can burn the damn thing.

"While that may be true," the *vasill* says, "dissolving a blood agreement is much more complex than dissolving a simple pledging."

"Bran!" My voice rises, near hysteria. "They can't do this."

"You can re-petition the court to dissolve the blood agreement," the *vasill* adds, "but that matter needs to be sent to the civil court and they're not open on Mondays."

Bran looks over the top of my head to his brother. He says something in French.

Damien responds the same.

They go back and forth over us ignoring the *vasill* as he drones on.

It's hard to tell what the Duval brothers are discussing. Their voices are even, their expressions distant, almost cold.

Out of the corner of my eye, I catch Bianca standing to her feet. Horror is rising on her face. It's the same expression a man might wear when he watches the ocean pull back right before a tsunami hits.

Bianca speaks French.

My stomach drops.

Oh shit.

"Damien!" she calls across the courtroom, "you can't—"

Damien and Bran are a blur.

The sound of cracking bone reaches my ears like a gunshot, but it isn't until the body hits the floor that I realize it's one of the guards.

I yelp in surprise.

A second guard drops.

The *vasill* drops next.

Julian's eyes burn bright blue, ready for war, but Julian isn't fast enough.

Julian isn't a Duval.

His head twists to an unnatural angle beneath the massive strength of Damien's capable hands.

One second Julian is snarling with rage and the next he's motionless on the marble floor.

"What the fuck?" The other vampire, the second councilman, kicks his chair back and lurches to his feet. "You can't do this."

"Yes, I fucking can." Damien crouches beside Julian's temporarily lifeless body and plucks the blood mate document from his pocket.

"You're going to start a war!"

Bran takes another step behind the bench. There is a hunger burning in his eyes that has nothing to do with blood and everything to do with carnage.

"Come on, man." The vampire backpedals. Bran advances. "Okay!" The man holds up his hands. "All right. Fuck, Duval. All this over some pussy?"

Bran's nostrils flare. His gaze is on the other vampire, but he says something in French.

Damien answers, "*Oui*," and Bran's hand sinks into the other vampire's chest and tears out his heart. Blood splatters across his face as his fangs turn razor sharp in his mouth.

Adrenaline rushes through my veins, sending a flash of warmth all through my body.

The councilman blinks at his heart in Bran's hand right before he bursts into ash.

The air goes still and silent. I can taste the cinders on the tip of my tongue.

Bran lets the heart drop from his grip and it bursts into ash mid-fall. He gives Bianca a quick tip of his chin and she races out of the room. The wolf shifter is already gone.

"Time to go," Damien says, his voice even and calm like they didn't just decimate an entire vampire court and start a war.

Bran comes over. There's a trail of blood from the bench to us where it dripped from his hand. Blood like bread crumbs. I can't seem to look away from it. I am entranced by it.

The brothers discuss something in French and Damien sweeps Kelly into the wide span of his arms.

"Wait, my sister—"

"Is coming with me," Damien says, barely looking at me, and they disappear from sight.

"Better if we go separately," Bran explains.

I don't move. I can't seem to move.

"What's wrong?" he asks.

"I...we..." Pinpricks of light dance in my eyes. My stomach is full of wings.

"It had to be done," Bran says. "Can you walk? If you can't, tell me now because we need to move."

How is he so calm?

"Mouse."

"Okay." I nod. "I can walk."

"Then go. *Now.*"

———

I don't know how we get out of the courthouse. It's all a dark blur.

One minute I'm staring at the blood on the marble floor and the next Bran is racing down a desolate street in the Bimmer.

The radio is off. It's just the silence and the pounding of my heart.

I want to crawl out of my skin.

"All of that was because of me."

"No," he corrects. "That's been meaning to happen for a very long time. Long before you."

"You just killed a vampire. Not like, pretend killed. Killed-*killed*."

He looks over at me briefly, the light of the dashboard liming him in an eerie glow. "Yes. And?"

"And he's dead. You tore out his heart."

He frowns, slightly exasperated with my need to state the obvious. "You wanted your sister, didn't you?"

"Yes, but—"

"No, mouse. You need to realize the gravity of what's happening here. Julian must know what you are and he's willing to use your sister against you to get to you. If we had let him walk out that door with Kelly, you might not have ever gotten her back. That needed to happen. It was unfortunate how it did, but I'm not going to dwell on the death of a vampire when he blatantly disrespected you."

"Who cares what some vampire says about me?" I mutter.

"I do, mouse. I fucking do."

I knew Bran was capable of violence. But up until now, I assumed, for the most part, that he followed the rules. All of this tonight—the court, the death, the blood—proves he doesn't.

His disregard for the rules is both frightening and fucking hot as hell.

Because Bran Duval doesn't give a fuck. He knows there are so few who could stand against him.

The power *is* intoxicating.

He is flesh and blood and walking fucking carnage.

And he's mine.

All fucking mine.

The headlights cut across a sharp turn in the road and Bran pushes the clutch and downshifts, the tendons in his forearm rising, flexing.

There's still blood coating his hand, drying in flakes around his fingernails.

The sight of it makes me yearn for something I have no name for.

Now I'm that man standing in front of a tidal wave.

"Stop the car."

He narrows his eyes. "Why?"

When I don't elaborate, he downshifts again and slows, steering the car onto the dirt shoulder.

I climb out and he meets me at the front and I jump into his arms without warning and he catches me easily, hands hooked around the backs of my thighs. I wrap my legs around his hips.

The wind picks up and the boughs of the hardwoods creak, the leaves rustling against one another.

"Thank you," I say to him, my hair hanging like a curtain around us. "Thank you for helping me save my sister."

"You don't have to thank me." He licks his bottom lip, his gaze going to my mouth. "I fucking enjoyed it."

I shiver beneath his words. "Even though it was terrifying, there was something overwhelmingly hot about it."

I would never admit that to anyone other than Bran, and I'm only just now realizing that the tingling I'd felt in my bones wasn't fear, but exhilaration.

And when I watched the blood drip from his hand,

distantly, in some far corner of my subconscious, something dark stirred.

"Wicked little mouse," he says with a growl.

I can feel him growing hard beneath the center of me. He drops me lower on his hips, rocking me against him and a thrill pulses through me.

I sink my mouth to his, claw my hands into his hair, trying to get closer. Never close enough.

Our breathing quickens. I slide my tongue over his and catch the sharp edge of a fang. Blood fills my mouth, coppery and sweet, and Bran whirls me around and slams me against the car door, ravenous for the taste.

"Fuck me," I say, panting against him.

He lowers me to the ground, wraps his hand around my neck. His grip is rough as his eyes burn in the night.

"Bend that ass over the hood then." His voice is raspy and thick. "And be quick about it, mouse."

Episode Thirty-Two

Wicked and Vile

I don't dawdle. I'm naked and bare for him in seconds. I don't even stop to think about the possibility that someone might drive by at any second and see me looking like a whore on the side of the road for one of the infamous Duval brothers.

I don't care. Because it's true.

I move to bend over the car, but Bran stops me.

"Hold on, little mouse." He hoists me up on the hood and I squeak from the shock of the cold metal on my ass. He hooks his hands around my thighs, yanking me to the edge with his vampire quickness. It happens so fast, my head spins.

"What are you doing?"

I would be lying if I said his promise from so many days ago to bend me over the hood of my car hasn't been ringing through my head like the distant toll of a bell.

He made me a promise.

He always sticks to his promises.

I'm not above pouting at this point.

The hunger in his eyes causes his irises to throb bright

orange. "I want to see what murder does to the taste of this pussy."

Before I can respond, he's covering me with his mouth.

Feeling him on me in that way, beneath those words, is a sensation I wasn't prepared for and I arch toward the sky.

Bran's mouth is clever, his tongue a master.

And of course.

Of course he knows how to treat a girl with his mouth.

My hands turn into claws and if I had sheets beneath me, they'd be fisted in my grip. Instead I scrabble at the cool metal and then satisfy my instinctual need to hang on to something by taking a fistful of Bran's hair.

"Oh fuck," I say through a moan as Bran laps me up.

He flicks at my clit, then dips to my opening and fucks me with his tongue.

"Well, well, little mouse," he says, his hot breath sending a new shiver to my core. "Murder makes you sweet."

It doesn't make sense, but the insinuation that I can be vile and wicked makes me fucking hotter than hell. My clit throbs as my nerves, lit like a firecracker, beg for release.

I tighten my hold on him and try to bring his mouth back to me, but he snatches both my wrists and forces me down, pinning me to the hood.

He tsk-tsks at me.

I close my eyes and exhale with frustration at the dark sky.

He's slower to taste me this time, dragging out the tortuous pleasure of his tongue on my wet pussy.

I buck as if that'll get me what I want and he nips at my thigh, causing me to squeal in pain.

There's the telltale sensation of blood welling from a puncture wound, dripping down the curve of my thigh to the swell of my ass.

Bran laps that up too.

"Stop punishing me," I say.

"Stop fighting me," he answers.

"I want you inside of me."

"And I want to hear you scream my name."

My breathing turns labored as my heart races in my ears.

Screaming doesn't come naturally to me.

I've always been afraid of my own voice.

Don't be loud.

Don't draw attention to yourself.

We're in the middle of nowhere. No one would hear me. Would they?

Bran flattens his tongue against me, tastes me long and deep and moans against me like I'm the sweetest thing he's ever put his mouth to.

It makes me feel like I'm made of starlight and honey. I tremble, squirm, and Bran tightens his hold on my wrists.

"Come for me, mouse."

"I want you to fuck me," I say.

"Oh, I will. But I'm fucking that tight little ass tonight and it's not going to be fun for you. Because I'm going to destroy it."

The sudden spike of fear blends with the pleasure in a riotous flutter in my belly.

I have my safe word.

I could use it if it got to be too much.

But...

But...

I want to be wicked and vile with Bran.

I want him to destroy me in all of his wicked and vile ways. Even if it hurts.

He returns to my pussy, works at my clit, and the wave builds at my sternum, and down through my belly.

I writhe on the hood.

Bran holds me down.

I'm just skin and nerves and blinding need.

He hits my swollen clit again and the wave cascades through me.

The stars in the sky blur into bright white smudges and I open my mouth and scream.

"Bran! Fuck. Oh fuck. Bran!"

He takes me through the wave, rides my pussy with his mouth as I buck beneath him, my body trying desperately to curl into itself. But he doesn't let me. He doesn't let up until I'm a puddle on the hood.

When he finally lets me go and straightens, dragging the back of his hand over his soaked chin, he smiles down at me with bright amber eyes. "That's a good girl."

I'm boneless.

Spent.

Satiated in a way that feels both liberating and gluttonous all at the same time.

Bran lifts me off the hood and puts me on my feet. He kisses me, giving me a taste of my own pleasure.

He's right—it does taste sweet.

His mouth travels to the curve of my neck, then up to my ear, his breath sending a warm shiver down my skin.

I can feel the hard press of him against my thigh.

His movements have grown frenzied, hungry.

I reach down between us and undo his pants, pulling him out.

As soon as my hand is wrapped around his cock, he growls deep in his chest, fangs sharpening in his mouth.

"If you only knew what you do to me, mouse..."

"I'd what?"

He licks his lips, looks down at me with heavy, glowing eyes. "You'd run."

My heart kicks up in my ears. "I'm not going anywhere."

"As if I'd let you."

Even though I just rode the biggest high on that orgasm,

my inner walls clench up at the reminder that he's claimed me as his.

As I stroke him, I can't help but watch his face, the way his mouth hardens and his jaw flexes, the way his Adam's apple sinks low in his throat. All of these little movements that add up to one thing—Bran Duval wants me.

He wants me as much as I want him and I've never been wanted in my entire life.

Pre-cum coats the head of his dick and I rub my thumb over the slit, then bring it to my mouth, suck it off. He growls again, nostrils flaring as his broad shoulders rise and fall with heightened breaths.

"You're not prepared for this, little mouse," he says.

"Yes, I am."

"No, you're not."

He brings his wrist to his mouth and bites into his own flesh. Blood coats his lips and drips from the wound.

I frown at him, unsure of what he means to do and then—

He holds his bleeding wrist over his cock, coating it in wet crimson. Fisting himself, he strokes long, once, twice.

He's using blood like lube.

Oh shit.

He spins me around, bends me over the hood and grabs my hips, forcing my ass up.

"Fuck, mouse. That tight little hole is just begging to be fucked."

I breathe out quickly.

He positions himself at my ass and I can feel the head swell against me, ready to plunge inside.

I hold my breath.

More blood slides down my seam, wetting our near joining.

If I wanted wicked and vile, I'm getting it.

He pushes in an inch, slow and steady, and I tense up.

Bran tightens his hold on my hips. "Breathe, mouse."

"I am."

"No, you're not."

I exhale, my breath fanning across the hood.

"That's a good girl."

He pushes in further, stretching me, and a squeak escapes me.

It feels like I'm being split in two. Stretched too thin. He's too big.

"Fuck, mouse. You're so fucking tight."

My chest fills with butterflies.

Another inch.

Another.

The wind shifts again and leaves skitter over the pavement and Bran Duval finally seats himself fully in my ass. He holds himself steady, the head of his cock swelling deep inside of me. "Remember your safe word."

"I will." My voice is too high-pitched and thin.

He pulls out, then slides back in and I clench against the sting.

"Mouse," he says on a groan.

I breathe hard, scrabbling at the hood as his pace picks up. He's enjoying it now and being used in this way makes me feel sickly satisfied.

This is the most illicit thing I've ever done and I don't want to like the way it makes me feel—not physically, not yet —*mentally*.

Does that make me wicked and vile?

Oh fuck.

Bran pumps faster, punishing me. His grip is bruising, his thrusts no longer gentle and I'm wetter than I've ever been as those satisfied wings take flight in my belly.

He's getting closer. I can tell by the tempo of his fucking, the rough groans, the hardness of his cock.

The in and out, in and out of his cock.

And I think I could come again.

I don't know how. I've never come twice in one go, but I'm primed, burning, clit throbbing.

I think I could.

I want to come while he fucks me this way.

I want to prove him wrong—this *is* fun for me even if it is painful.

Whatever dark thing stirred inside of me at that courthouse is now ravenous for more.

I reach down between my legs and take command of my own pleasure.

The beat of the orgasm flashes through me like oil in fire —quick and hot and consuming. I cry out and my voice bounces off of the hood of the car and echoes in the forest and Bran pumps deep, spilling hot cum in my ass.

"*Fuck, mouse.*" He slides out, shoves back in, the head of his cock throbbing at my center. He stays buried for several beats and I collapse against the car, legs shaking. And when he finally pulls out of me, I twist and slide down to the ground and hang my head back against the tire.

Bran drops beside me and takes my hand in his.

When I turn to him, there's a noticeable pinch around his eyes.

"What are you thinking?" I ask.

I want to know the intimate details of what's inside his head. I want to know him like no one else does. Because in the end, it won't be the fucking or the violence that makes what we have special, it'll be the quiet moments like this when no one is looking, when he tells me his secrets and I guard them with my heart.

"Sometimes I'm afraid I'll break you," he admits. He reaches over with his other hand and pushes aside a lock of hair that's stuck in the sweat on my cheek. "I will always be a little sadistic and you will always be breakable and so devastatingly beautiful it makes me ache."

Tears immediately well in my eyes. I don't know what to do with this compliment. It feels too big to hold.

He stands up and gently hoists me to stand beside him. He takes my face in his hands. There's firelight in his irises as he says, "I was turned too young to know what it means to love with a mortal heart, but if I had to guess, this must be pretty fucking close."

"Are you saying that you lo—"

He clamps his hand over my mouth, snuffing out the word before it finds air.

"Don't."

I dare not move.

"Don't say it, mouse."

I give him a quick nod. When he pulls his hand back, satisfied that I'll obey, I have to ask.

"Why not?"

He glances away from me, his gaze going to the dark horizon of the back road. "Because it fucking terrifies me." When he meets my eyes again, there's no glow to his irises. Just a hooded darkness. "And it should terrify you too."

He scoops up my clothes and helps me dress even though I'm an absolute fucking mess and desperately need a shower.

Our drive back to Duval House is comfortably silent, but Bran's grip on the stick shift is white-knuckled the whole way there.

Episode Thirty-Three

Bloody Glory

Bran is quiet on the drive back to Duval House. Quiet and distant. He parks beneath the *porte cochère* and hands the keys off to a girl who avoids his eyes. He doesn't say a word to her or me as he guides me through the house and toward the back where French doors lead to what looks like a courtyard.

Something is wrong. But I don't know how to help him.

Right now, I can sense his energy literally vibrating through his body. I don't think now is the time to have a conversation, but I'm not going to let us go to bed without tackling it.

Because we have to talk about it. We have to talk about all of it.

"Jimmy," Bran says.

Jimmy appears within seconds. She's wearing the most adorable denim overalls rolled at the ankles. She's barefoot with paint splattered across her toes and smudged across the front pocket of the overalls. Her arrival disrupts the air around us and she brings with her the scent of something woody and floral.

"Hi," she says and looks from me back to Bran. I've noticed Jimmy is always watching Bran when she's near, like a snake charmer might watch a snake, making sure it isn't ready to strike.

I don't know what their relationship is, but Bran did admit that he'd die for Jimmy. I think Jimmy might feel the same way about him.

I would be lying if I said that didn't stir a little bit of envy. Jimmy clearly knows him better than I do and I have a lot of ground to cover to even match her depth of knowing.

"Take my little mouse to the Anneliese," Bran says.

I have no idea what that is.

"Show her to a shower and get her some clean clothes."

"Wait, where are you going?" I grab his arm, feeling him pull away from me. Last time I was left alone in Duval House, Sky sought me out and turned everything upside down.

It's hard to say how she feels about me now.

"I have to see my brother," Bran answers. "The Anneliese will keep you safe. And so will Jimmy."

Jimmy nods.

"Clean up, mouse," he adds with a smug grin.

I'm a mess, covered in blood and cum. I desperately need a shower and the promise of one has me salivating. But...I don't want him to leave either.

"I'll be back soon," he says and slides his hand around my neck, dragging me in. The kiss he plants on my forehead is featherlight, but his grip is firm and I want to melt beneath the pressure.

But then he's pulling away.

Jimmy rushes ahead to stop him and the two exchange words. They're nothing more than a whisper and I can't hear what's said.

When Jimmy turns back to me, Bran is already gone.

"I'm sorry," I say.

"For what?"

"Well, because you're babysitting me again."

She reaches out for one of the handles on the French doors. "Do you think the secret service rolls their eyes every time they're tasked with guarding someone?"

Jimmy gestures for me to head outside and we walk into an open-air courtyard beneath the starlit sky.

"I'm not the president of the United States."

"No, but you're valued by Bran. That makes you important. I have a duty to this house and to Damien and Bran. I don't care what the task is. I'll do it."

She walks ahead of me on the stone-paved path. It's a short walk through well-tended flowering bushes. Soft solar lights illuminate the path and somewhere to my left, a water feature gurgles in the dark.

We stop beneath the overhanging roof of a building separate from Duval House.

"Is this the Anneliese?" I ask.

Jimmy nods and punches a code into a digital panel beside the door. The panel beeps and a deadbolt clanks open.

"It's deeded to a human who doesn't live anywhere near here. Only Bran, Damien, and myself have been invited."

"Why's it called the Anneliese?"

We step inside. The air is cool and smells clean.

"It's named after Damien and Bran's little sister."

"They have a sister?"

"Had," Jimmy corrects.

"Oh god. That's..."

"A long story," she finishes.

"Right. Of course."

The Anneliese is open floor plan in the front. Directly to my left is a dining table nestled in a room done entirely in glass. Even though it's dark, I can tell the room is surrounded in greenery outside so that it must feel like you're dining in the forest.

There's a kitchen to the far left, and a living room to the far right, with a cozy seating area directly to the right of the front door.

A wide hallway runs through the center of the house and appears to break off left and right at the end.

"Come this way," Jimmy says. "Bran's room is down here. There's an attached bathroom."

"Is my sister here?" I ask.

"Yes, but I believe she's already sleeping. She'll be in Damien's room down the hall if you want to check in on her."

I eye the closed door. "No, that's all right. She's been through a lot in the last twenty-four hours. Better to let her rest."

But I'm so damn relieved we're beneath the same roof, protected by the Duvals.

We enter Bran's room. This is...what, the third place of his I've been to in so many days? There are more black and white photographs hung on the wall. The bedding is an exact match to the bedding he has at the house next to ours.

It's so decidedly him that it makes me immediately feel at home.

"Shower is through there." Jimmy points at a closed door to the left of the bed. "I'll get you some clothes and will leave them on the end of the bed."

"Thanks, Jimmy."

She gives my shoulder a squeeze. "Don't mention it."

When she leaves me, I strip off my clothes, toss them in the trash, and immediately jump into the shower. God, the hot water feels amazing. I'm learning to accept that being around Bran will always be bloody, but damn if my germaphobe OCD-self isn't crying a little inside.

As promised, I find folded clothes waiting for me on the

end of the bed. There's a pair of sleep shorts made of soft linen and a tank top and panties. Jimmy has found me a lounge bra, but I go without.

Once I'm clean and dressed, I pace the hallway outside the room. I find Jimmy keeping watch in the sitting area, giving her a clear view of Duval House and the courtyard. She's reading a book and gives me a smile when I come out.

"How long do you think Bran will be?" I ask. It's nearing 4 am now. Where the hell is he?

"With Bran and Damien, it's always hard to tell," Jimmy responds. "I haven't heard anything to cause me to worry."

"Okay. Will you let me know if you do?"

"Of course."

What if they went to confront Julian? I'm sure he's up and on his feet now, having healed from the broken neck.

I bet he's burning with rage.

Can Bran and Damien take him and Locke House? I'm sure they can but not if they're ambushed.

Bran better be okay, goddamn it. Just thinking about something happening to him makes my stomach knot up.

I busy myself with a glass of water from the kitchen, then get nosy at the bookshelves in the living room as I wait. I spend a half hour flicking through a book about eighteenth century France until I can't stop yawning and decide to give in.

"Goodnight, Jimmy," I call.

She looks up from her book. "Night. Let me know if you need me."

In the bedroom, I climb in beneath the soft sheets of Bran's bed and am disappointed they don't smell like him. My eyes are burning I'm so tired, but I can't sleep. I toss and turn. The digital clock on the dresser says it's after five now. The sun will be up soon.

Where is he?

Finally, I hear the front door click closed and the air part in the bedroom a second later.

"Bran?" I ask the dark.

"I'm here, little mouse." His voice is hoarse and quiet.

"Where have you been? I've been worried." I slip from the bed and reach over to click on the bedside lamp. "You could have call—"

Light fills the room and I catch sight of him.

He's covered in blood.

So much blood.

"What happened?" I rush over to him, the panic tightening like a band across my chest. "Are you hurt?"

"It's not mine," he says.

"Then who—Julian?"

He ignores me and goes to the bathroom and starts stripping, adding his bloody clothes to the pile of mine in the trash can.

It's been a bloody, violent night.

"The who doesn't matter," he answers once he's standing naked in front of me.

I can't help but drag my eyes over his body. The blood is still splattered on his neck and over his face. It coats his arms and has dried on his hands. But the rest of him is clean.

God, he is so fucking hot.

He's got abs for days and those shadowed lines that arch over his hips and run to a V right down to his cock.

He's not hard, but he's still big and I have the urge to take him in my hand.

He tsk-tsks at me, clearly scenting the stirring of my arousal, and it's becoming my new favorite thing. It makes me feel naughty when he does it.

"Are you okay?" I ask him, echoing Jimmy's earlier question that he so artfully dodged.

"Of course I am."

"You were distant when you left and now this." I gesture at him.

"Damien and I went for a hunt."

I don't even want to ask for the details. It's better if I don't know.

He comes over to me and I backpedal into the tiled wall next to the vanity. A startled little breath escapes me. "I've been thinking," I say. "There's something I want to get out." My heart picks up its tempo. "You keep telling me to find my voice. So I need you to listen."

"I'm listening."

"I'm not afraid of you."

"Your heart rate says otherwise."

I swallow, licking my lips. Bran towers over me, naked and intimidating.

"I'm not afraid that you'll hurt me," I correct. "If I use the safe word, I know you'll listen and I'm not worried about what comes after. I don't think you're going anywhere and I'm not either. I have faith in you. I trust you. And you have to trust me when I say I know what I want. So stop telling me I should be terrified of you and stop telling me I should be afraid of how I feel or how you feel or what we—"

He kisses me, long and slow, his tongue sliding over mine, his bloody hand on my throat.

Butterflies fill my stomach as he breathes out through his nose, almost like a sigh.

When he pulls back, his eyes are glowing. "Now it's time you listen."

I swallow hard. This better not be a rejection or I swear to god—

"I love you, Jessie."

My heart stops beating.

I just blink up at him, on the verge of screaming or sobbing. Not out of fear, but triumph, relief.

He said it.

He said it.

My eyes turn watery and when I blink several tears escape.

Bran reaches over and swipes them away.

"I will never leave your side. Feel safe in using your safe word should you need it." He smirks and tucks a lock of my hair behind my ear. "I can control myself, even around that tight little ass."

I laugh and duck my head. Heat rises in my cheeks.

"I am your knight," he goes on. "Your protector. I'll even be your vampire boyfriend if it pleases you. And while I don't think you fully understand what you've gotten yourself into, I am yours, in all of my bloody glory."

I smile and look down at his glory.

He's semi-hard, growing harder by the second. I instinctively reach down to touch him, but he bats me away. "I will bow at your feet," he says, "but you'll still obey me. And you'll only get this cock when I say you get this cock."

I pout up at him. "Then say I get it."

"Absolutely not. You need to rest. I fucked that ass hard."

"Stop talking about my ass."

"Why?"

"Because it makes me blush."

"I know. It's adorable."

I rake my teeth over my bottom lip, trying not to smile about it. "But I'm fae, remember. Which means I heal quickly, it seems. Which explains why my entire life, I never had to go to the hospital and—"

Bran pulls me back toward the bedroom. "I'm taking a shower and you're going to bed." He tucks me into the sheets.

"Fine. But hurry," I say up to him.

"I'll only be a minute." He flicks off the light. The shower turns on a few seconds later.

I lay there, eyes wide open, waiting for him to come to bed.

So much has changed. So much is yet to come.

The room is dark, but beyond it, I know the sun is rising, which means it's Monday, the day before my birthday and my Pledge.

How will I sleep at all before then?

But as soon as Bran comes to bed and slips in behind me, wraps me in his arms and surrounds me with his scent, I give in to the exhaustion and fall quickly to sleep, warm in the knowledge that Bran Duval loves me.

He fucking loves me.

――――

You can keep reading Hot Vampire right now on Kindle Vella!

Pick up where you left off with episode 34 to find out what happens next for Jessie and her hot vampire.

Start Episode 34 now so you don't miss out!

For international readers, you can keep reading on Patreon right here: https://www.patreon.com/nikkistcrowe

――――

Want to get inside Bran Duval's head and find out how he really feels about Jessie?

Read a bonus episode that takes place between episode 32 and 33 and is told from Bran's POV!

Start reading now!
https://www.subscribepage.com/nikkistcrowebonus

———

**WANT TO JOIN OTHER HOT VAMPIRE READERS TO
DISCUSS ALL THINGS BRAN AND JESSIE?**

Come join the reader group Nikki St. Crowe's Nest on
Facebook!
https://www.facebook.com/groups/nikkistcrowesnest/

Also by Nikki St. Crowe

Wrath & Rain Trilogy

Ruthless Demon King

Sinful Demon King

Vengeful Demon King

Vicious Lost Boys

The Never King

Cursed Vampires

A Dark Vampire Curse

Midnight Harbor

Hot Vampire Next Door (ongoing Vella serial)

Hot Vampire Next Door: Season One (ebook)

Hot Vampire Next Door: Season Two (ebook)

Hot Vampire Next Door: Season Three (ebook)

About the Author

Nikki St. Crowe has been writing for as long as she can remember. Her first book, written in the 4th grade, was about a magical mansion full of treasure. While she still loves writing about magic, she's ditched the treasure for something better: villains, monsters, and anti-heroes, and the women who make them wild.

These days, when Nikki isn't writing or daydreaming about villains, she can either be found on the beach or at home with her husband and daughter.

Exclusive Member's Only Access
https://www.subscribepage.com/nikkistcrowe

Follow Nikki on TikTok
https://www.tiktok.com/@nikkistcrowe

Gain early access to cover reveals and sneak peeks on Nikki's Patreon:
https://www.patreon.com/nikkistcrowe

Join Nikki's Reader Group
Nikki St. Crowe's Nest
https://www.facebook.com/groups/nikkistcrowesnest/

Visit Nikki on the web at:
www.nikkistcrowe.com

Printed in Great Britain
by Amazon